Suspect, Love

A Profound Abysm

Judith D. Andrade

authorHOUSE®

AuthorHouse™
1663 Liberty Drive
Bloomington, IN 47403
www.authorhouse.com
Phone: 1-800-839-8640

Published by AuthorHouse 4/17/2013

ISBN: 978-1-4567-3764-1 (sc)
ISBN: 978-1-4567-3763-4 (e)

Library of Congress Control Number: 2011902133

Images provided by Bryan Davies Photos, Creemore ON
and licensed for single use by Judith D. Andrade

This book is printed on acid-free paper.

Dedication and thanks

Nothing ever occurs in isolation. I give thanks to all the wonderful people who have passed through my life in one way or another. Many of you have left something special with me in your words or actions. Although my characters are fictional, their stories are a blend of all those experiences. For a long time I was privileged to work at The Doctor's Hospital in Toronto. My former colleagues were a dedicated group of doctors and nurses whose commitment to improving the quality of life was the cornerstone of their work. I dedicate this book to them.

Lisa, was a delightful child, whose big heart and wordless love was a beacon of light to everyone who knew her. I give thanks for the joy that she and her family brought into my life for seventeen years. My thanks also to Gyma, whose personal life struggle served as my role model for courage. Each of their individual journeys, into the Summerland of final rest, gave me the impetus to fulfill the promise of writing from my heart.

My gratitude goes out to my sister Gertrude King who continues to help edit my stories and offer advice which I value and also her husband Bryan Davies whose storytelling photography graces the front and back cover of this book.

Last but by no means least, I appreciate the patience of my long suffering husband Harold, my two sons and my five grandchildren, who put up with my intellectual absences from their lives while I am writing. To their credit, they support me in everything I do just the same.

Because all of them have touched my life and made it special, I suspect love, is the driving force which binds us all together.

Suspect, Love
A Profound Abysm
Author: Judith D. Andrade

Basilica, Italy, 1982

Giovanna woke up with a pounding headache, immediately sensing a change in her environment. She waited and waited, listening intently before it became clear that the earth beneath the house was shifting. It had been years since there was an earthquake in the region, although the threat was always present. Giovanna's advanced state of pregnancy seemed to make her more sensitive to atmospheric changes.

Reaching out a trembling hand, she touched her husband Mateo, urging him to wake up. Bleary eyed he turned over, thinking that his wife was ready to give birth. It only took a few seconds for him to realize that a disaster was looming. Jumping out of bed, he felt the earth continue to quiver beneath his feet. Shaking off the last of his fogginess, Mateo helped his wife up and escorted her down the short flight of stairs to the front door.

The small house, one of several crowded into a small village, could withstand much, but no one ever knew the extent of damage which could follow the uprising of earth's energy. Many other families, living in the shadow of Mt. Etna, were also moving out of their homes. Mateo settled his wife gently near the centre of the road which ran through town.

Mindful of her delicate condition and hating to leave, he none the less stepped back into the house.

His aging parents needed help to get up. They would have trouble finding their way in the darkness. Going outside was a precautionary action. Falling beams were sometimes more dangerous than the tremors. So far, Mateo didn't feel anything too alarming but it was wise not to take chances. The conscientious but cautious man checked to see if there was any obvious damage in the lower part of the house. Once satisfied that everything was intact, he made his way to the small blocked off corner, on the ground floor, where his parents slept.

The elderly couple, who had eight other children, had welcomed their youngest son back home just over two years ago. They helped to provide Mateo, his wife and invalid daughter with a home. Their son lost his job following a wrenching shoulder injury on board the ship where he had worked for years. The healing was long and painful. Even a job as simple as picking fruits or olives was out of the question. He had been unable to find much else. Mateo often travelled far from home in search of something manageable. The most recent return to the village of his birth only resulted in an unexpected pregnancy. Unfortunately, adding another child only increased the burden on the limited resources of the cash strapped family.

Mateo listened for any warning sounds as he also turned anxious thoughts to his young daughter. Anunziata was not a strong child. Not long after her birth, the Doctor told the shocked parents that she had a bad heart and could not live long unless she could get life saving surgery. Such an expensive procedure was out of the question for the family. Giovanna and Mateo had neither funds to travel to the nearest hospital capable of such surgery, nor money to pay the Surgeon who might be able to save her. Despite her many limitations, Anunziata was a loving, intuitive child. Her physical organ may be weak, but her spiritual heart was beautiful. The couple, saddened by the plight of their child, was determined to provide a loving home in which she would thrive according to God's will. A gentle giving nature endeared her to everyone.

Praying that Anunziata was still asleep, Mateo went into his parent's room first, waking the elderly couple gently and shepherding them out of the house to stand with his wife. The rumblings increased slightly. Other families were getting up and leaving their homes, gathering in the lanes, hopeful that the great Mount Etna would be satisfied with a small sacrifice on the part of her devoted tenants. Mateo went back into the house, entering his daughter's small bedroom upstairs. He whispered softly and gathered her into his arms, continuing to talk in a reassuring way. She wrapped her tiny arms around his neck, knowing without being told that the mountain was making its presence felt.

'Be careful Papa. Don't fall,' she admonished in her sweet voice. Holding him tightly, Anunziata said nothing more knowing that her father's painful shoulder was aching even as he lifted the feather light body. He carefully put his foot down on the first step. Unexpectedly, a tremulous wave rumbled beneath the village. Screams could be heard in the distance. Some crockery fell to the floor. Mateo pushed his back against the wall for added support. He held tightly to his child. Within seconds, the quiet was as eerie as the previous noise. Moving carefully, Mateo reached the front door. He set his daughter at the side of the road next to her nervous mother. He breathed deeply while rubbing an aching shoulder. Seeing his family safe was satisfying. He hoped that any further tremors would be minor so they could soon return to their beds.

Nothing happened for several moments. Everyone began to whisper, relief animating their voices. Even though the tension began to ease, no one was willing to actually step forward and go back inside their homes. Neighbours shared opinions back and forth as they waited. Hardly a soul, in that small village, could remember much more of the night's events. When the deep rent in the earth had travelled its course through the street, the missing and the dead were counted in at least half of every family. Long after the ground lay quiet, the screams could still be heard echoing symbolically off the sides of the mountain.

Giovanna, who had been studying the actions of her kind and gentle husband as he stood immobile and watchful over his family, suddenly opened her mouth in horror. Within a heartbeat of the massive split, Mateo had stumbled back near the edge of the precipice. Wheeling his arms around, the frightened man tried to right his body. The movement of his shoulder brought a moment of excruciating pain, tipping him further back.

Time seemed to hold itself in abeyance for a breathless moment. Giovanna could not stretch out her arm. The oversized belly slowed her down. Had she put out her hand, they would have both gone, buried together forever. Instead, she saw the aging father reach out to grab his son, but the effort to save Mateo's life only pulled them both into the gaping hole.

Giovanna would not remember whether she screamed from fear, loss or incredible pain as something heavy landed on her leg. At the final, wrenching crack of the bone, she knew nothing more.

∞

Hours later, rescue workers found a pregnant woman struggling to call out as she drifted in and out of consciousness. Soft whimpers quickly drew them to her side. It was clear that she was in labour. Without a second thought, they gathered her battered body aboard a make-shift stretcher and moved her to a waiting ambulance. It was many more hours before another group of men, searching in the rubble for other survivors, approached the body of a young girl. Her hand was entwined with an older woman.

'She's gone Mark, but the old woman looks like she might still be alive.'

Anunziata did not understand the words. She barely felt the hand which struggled to release her from her grandmother's death grip. By sheer will, she moved her lips, blue and stiff, not from death but from the heart condition which weakened her body. Desperation for their situation and fear for the safety of her mother had set her dysfunctional heart pounding. Shocked into a life saving rhythm by the unexpected movement, her nearly lifeless body was raised from the dirt and stones by the Canadian rescuers. The men were clearly surprised to find anyone else alive. By that time there were many more helpers. The transportation needed to take the injured to makeshift hospitals was readily available.

The efficient and experienced doctor, who had volunteered to be part of the rescue team was surprised to see an uninjured, but desperately sick child brought to his tent. He checked her over and over, looking for some sign of internal bleeding which would justify her extremely pale complexion. There was none. Puzzled, he searched for a local interpreter who could speak with the young child. Gentle questions yielded nothing. She had no pain, just a deep sadness for the loss of her mother and father.

As more and more equipment became available, the x-ray evidence of her diminished capacity was clear. A few more tests revealed an astonishing fact. She had survived well beyond a normal life expectancy with a heart which functioned completely backwards! Dr. Glen Senimot was strangely inspired by Anunziata and stepped out of his comfort zone to make a few phone calls. He was modestly unaware of the admiration and respect of his colleagues towards his unselfish work. As far as he was concerned, the best paediatric surgeons in the world worked between the children's hospital in Toronto and its adjacent adult counterpart. How quickly he was put through, surprised him.

∞

Toronto, Ontario

Angus Howard sat at the oak desk in his small office. As a senior resident he was among the privileged few who were provided with real working space. Because of his exceptional marks, he had been chosen to spend the last few months of his residency working with the world class pediatric cardiologist who headed the department. Dr. Larry Silverberg was an amazing diagnostician and surgeon. He had much to teach those who would follow his footsteps. Angus felt honored to work with him. The dedicated doctor did not, however, feel lucky about the bills facing him in the future. He had massive debts to pay off. His education had been expensive and worth every penny but only if he could establish a thriving practice once his pediatric fellowship was complete.

Open and unread on his desk was a large book outlining the complex types of congenital heart disease, known to afflict the newborn. As interesting as it was, the small savings summarized on his bank statement did not balance well with the pile of bills awaiting his attention. He was tempted to push the book aside and focus attention on his debts. A phone call interrupted his reverie.

'Dr. Howard, can you take an urgent long distance call for Dr. Silverberg? He's out for the morning.'

The crisp voice of the secretary penetrated Angus' trance-like state. 'I'll take it,' he replied quickly.

'It's Dr. Glen Senimot. He's calling from Italy.'

Angus was surprised. The modest humanitarian was highly regarded and famous for his work in troubled communities. Everyone was aware of the major disaster in Italy and knew that he would be working there, in the heart of it, trying to save lives. '*Strange that he was calling!*' A line of concern appeared between Angus' brows. He made his own position clear before listening to the horrific story of devastation and the reason for the call. Dr. Senimot, trying to talk on a makeshift phone amidst heartbreaking sounds of suffering, quickly got to the point.

'This orphaned girl is uninjured but she has a congenital heart condition which I am unable to properly diagnose or treat in these conditions. What makes this case different is her longevity. I have never known a child to survive beyond infancy.'

The spiritual quality which endeared the humanitarian to the world was evident in his next words.

'There is something about her which pulls at my own heartstrings. She is unique Dr. Howard. How she survived this mess, I don't know. We feel obliged to do something to help. If Dr. Silverberg is willing to accept her, I will see what I can do to get her over.'

The words and tone of voice had a compelling quality which could not be ignored. After hearing the story of the orphan, Angus could almost feel the same pull on his own battered and bruised heartstrings, although he could not have said why. He looked down at the small savings in his account. His hesitation was so slight as to be almost indistinguishable from a normal breath.

'I'll take responsibility for this. If you can get her safely on a plane, then do so. I have some friends who will help.'

'I'll get in touch with the embassy today. Thank you, Dr. Howard.'

Angus pushed the pile of bills to one side and drew the book in front of his face searching the index for a particular topic. '*Transposition of the Great Vessels. I'd better get my facts straight if I am going put my career on the line to advocate for her.*'

Chapter 1

Toronto, 1994

Rosanna quickened her pace down the dark corridor as the pager beeped again. The eerie sound echoed off the walls. 'I'm coming' she muttered to no one in particular. Despite her overall diminutive stature, long legs quickly ate up the distance. The aging downtown hospital had not been designed for easy access between units.. *'A golf cart would have been handy,'* she thought, hating the aching calves which seemed to reach maximum discomfort in the early hours of the morning.

Unafraid, despite numerous stories of ghost sightings, the young night supervisor chose the basement corridor as the fastest route. Ahead of her, she could see the shadows of the low level night lights beaming down. Rosanna climbed the short two flights of stairs and pushed open the double doors separating the Paediatric unit from the Obstetrical suite. She was greeted by a frazzled looking night nurse.

'Thank God you're on tonight. It just seems like one crisis

after another. Things sure ain't getting any better.' It was clear the night charge nurse was stressed. Rosanna observed her carefully, noting that her hands were swift and sure, checking names and dosages against the medication record sheet. Mentally, Rosanna tried to sort through the numerous tasks which would be needing attention on the busy unit.

'Give me a quick rundown of what needs to be done, Margaret.' The experienced supervisor used an economy of words hoping not to increase the obvious tension emanating from the nurse.

'What doesn't need to be done? I am behind on my meds already and that one over there... is all over my case because I can't run to assist him the minute he comes in. Does he think he's the only one who has work to do?'

Rosanna's eyes followed the direction of the head tilt. The partially glass encased resuscitation room was located at the far end of the unit. A unidentifiable care provider, dressed in green scrubs, was observing a baby, who was lying immobile on an over-bed warmer. He seemed more intent on the tiny patient than harassing the night nurses. Rosanna did not make any rejoinder. Tension between nurses and medical staff was a long standing issue. She turned away from the tall figure before trying again to get a sense of where she could help.

'What's your major concern right now? I'm not able to do your medications but maybe something else?'

'Cory in 203 was screaming so much his stitches popped. The resident is working with Lou to stop the bleeding. He'll be going to the OR as soon as the surgeon comes in. Ping is specialing a post op gastric insertion tube. Just as we got that sorted out, ..uh...the baby over there, suddenly had an increase in his respiratory distress. It was a good thing…*he* came up but, he's oh..sooo, demanding. I can't be everywhere.'

The young nurse, simmering with anger or resentment, increased her tempo, quickly pulling vials from the cupboard, drawing up injections for her patients, labelling and sorting them into different piles for distribution. She still had not gotten to the point. The night supervisor, on a tight schedule of her own, was beginning to feel some of that frustration.

'Do you want me to help him?' Rosanna asked quietly inclining her head in the direction of the tall figure.

'Would you Ms. Amadeo? You are really great you know. None of the ….'

'Just tell me what I need, and then you can get back to your meds.'

'Since you are not wearing a uniform, you'll have to cap, gown and mask after you scrub up over there. Dr. Howard will have a tray at the bedside with everything on it if he needs to intubate. Are you're ok with that?' Margaret, a fiery red head, with a legendary temper looked up then realizing that the procedure may not be familiar to supervisory staff working in the office.

'Sure. I'm fine assisting with the procedure.'

Rosanna hurried over to a nearby sink to quickly prepare herself. She removed her lab coat, tucked her shoulder length, raven hair in a soft OR cap, and slipped on a mask. She put on the protective gown and washed her hands. As night supervisor, she wasn't required to wear a uniform but all too often she found it necessary to help out on the busy wards. She knew most of her colleagues would probably have looked for another nurse on a less busy ward, but the staff resented being moved from one place to another mid shift. Sometimes, the RN would lack the speciality skills required on other units despite being competent on their own. Rosanna wasted little time in getting ready. Her own work would have to wait.

'What can I do to help?' she whispered softly approaching the bed. Rosanna could tell at a quick glance that the little boy, struggling for breath, was in serious trouble. The Doctor bending over him was trying to fill the baby's tortured lungs with air. He was using a bag and mask attached to an oxygen outlet and pressure gauge. His long fingers wrapped easily around the little body with all the gentleness in the world.

'Look Mrs. DaSilva, your son is having some difficulty breathing right now. I know you're worried but it would be better if you waited outside. A nurse will be along in a minute.' His voice was soothing and very reassuring. Rosanna was impressed but quickly made her own position clear.

'I'm not the boy's mother. I'm here to…'

'I don't care why you're here,' he interrupted rudely. 'I need a nurse. If you want to help, then see what's keeping her or the Respiratory Therapist. This child's condition is not improving. I am going to have to intubate him before he can be transferred to Paediatric ICU. If no one is available on the unit, call a code pink!'

Rosanna inwardly bristled at the tone, but kept her irritation to a minimum. Awareness of the situation was weighing heavily on her. 'I **am** a nurse, I know CPR, and I'm here to help.'

'Why didn't you say so? Grab this bag, air pressures at 7. I am just going to get things ready, then insert the tracheal tube.' His voice was as crisp and precise as his actions.

Rosanna did little more than nod. It had been awhile since she was needed to help with such a small infant. She watched intently as he prepared the instruments. This was no novice Doctor. His hands moved over the tray with speed and accuracy, picking out the essential equipment.

'Two weeks old, readmission, septic, decreasing oxygen saturation, poor air entry. 'When I am ready to insert, I want you to stand by with the ventilator attachments. I have already preset the machine. He's poorly oxygenated. Seconds count. Keep an eye on the monitor and read out his heart rate if it drops below 90.

Rosanna's hand was steady. She had worked in a neonatal unit for almost two years at another large tertiary hospital. She knew what to expect. The doctor had twenty seconds to get the tube in.

'OK now….let's go!'

'Heart rate 88!'

'Damn!' His expletive was a clear indicator of a rough start. 'Pass the forceps!'

'Heart rate 84!'

'Light, Suction, tube,' The hands moved quickly.

'Heart rate 78!'

'Come on little one. Easy, easy son, we'll be done in a second.'

It was hard to believe the softly spoken words came from the same man.

'Heart rate 74!'

'Suction again'

'Heart rate 68.'

'That's it…ventilator quickly.'

Rosanna breathed a sigh of relief. She was impressed by the doctor's speed. It was always harrowing to insert an airway tube on a very ill baby. The procedure was so stressful. It didn't take long for some colour to come back into the blue tinged lips. The heart rate began a steady climb upwards. She observed every action taken by the doctor and admitted to herself that he was exceptionally skilled, at least when handling this crisis. His hands and voice had been soft, almost tender.

'I'm just going to give him a mild sedative. He was getting very restless from the lack of oxygen.' Sure hands quickly drew up a drug from the medication cart and injected it into an IV line.

'Give me the name and the dosage of the medications you've given so I can chart the information for the staff.'

He halted his activity for a brief second before changing tone again. 'Aren't you staff? I thought you said you were a nurse?'

'Of course I am but…I..' She turned away to place the used instruments on the tray.

'Wait a minute. You're not wearing a uniform. What's going

on here?' The long fingers held the tube in place as he looked up briefly. It was just enough time for him to see Rosanna's street clothes at the open back of her gown. He put tape in place to secure the tracheal tube and straightened up.

'I am going to report this to the nursing authority. We can't have just anyone assisting with highly technical patient care.'

'Report what you like. My name is Ms. Amadeo and I am a nurse. I told you that already. Now, if you will tell me the name of the drug you are giving, I will pass it on to Margaret who seems to be on her way over with the RT.'

Rosanna quickly wrote the name and dosage on a piece of paper before passing it to the nurse.

'He has intubated the baby and given this medication. Is everything alright with the other little boy Margaret?' Rosanna's tone was tight.

'Yes, he's gone to the OR. Lou's back and Jorge will help me take this little guy up to PICU. If you could just write a short note on the chart, we should be fine now. Thanks a lot Ms. Amadeo. I'll page again if we need more help.'

Rosanna did her charting and left the unit, head held high. Margaret easily picked up the tension at the bedside. Her 'I told you so' look wasn't missed. None the less, Rosanna refused to acknowledge it. She was fuming as she hurried down the hall. There were several more units to check and her night reports to complete before she went off duty.

∞

'Why didn't you take that emergency call on pediatrics Colleen?' Rosanna asked wearily dropping into the wooden chair behind the aging oak desk.

'You were closer weren't you?'

'Yes, I might have been….but you are much more familiar with the ward than I am."

'Those girls don't seem to be able to manage. In my day, we had more patients and less staff. We didn't have supervisors to call every minute to help. They should learn to pace themselves better. Every little emergency flusters them.' The words weren't harsh, just coldly matter of fact but there was an element of thinly veiled disgust.

'This was a major ….no..... two emergencies.'

'Then you were the best person to be there. That's what this modern training is all about; learning to delegate, not learning to be a good nurse.'

Rosanna sighed and stood up. 'My feet really hurt. Is there any coffee left?'

'Can't bear to hear the truth, eh little girl?'

Colleen's tone was gruffly affectionate but Rosanna chose to ignore the jibe as she poured some lukewarm, barely recognizable, beverage in a cup before resuming her seat. She had been working with the senior supervisor for over two years. Most nights there was a major or minor point of conflict between them. It was always the same *old vs. new* in nursing. Rosanna was sick and tired of the recurring theme and said so, with increasing frequency.

'You young people are always tired. If you ever knew what

we had to do without all the fancy equipment that you have now. Well, it doesn't bear thinking about.' Without an immediate response to her baiting, Colleen continued. 'What would you know about the old ways anyhow?'

'I've lived with it all my life. When my father came to this country he made a new life for himself, found a job and started a family. It wasn't easy but he hung on fiercely to his old Sicilian values as a stabilizing factor in a strange and often unfriendly new culture.'

'That's your dad Annie, not you!' Colleen interjected before continuing. 'You have a Masters degree. That makes you very much a woman of today.'

Rosanna wasn't daunted by the finality of the words or the implied criticism of being highly educated in a profession which also required exceptional practical skills.

'It didn't come easily. Papa felt that educating a woman was a waste of time. Even though I was a straight A student, I had to fight all the time for the right to attend University, yet he sent my older brother willingly…and….' she paused to take a deep breath, emotion making her words defiant, '…..and even though he finally gave in, nursing was the only program he would allow me to take at McMaster.'

'I suppose that you are going to tell me he wanted you barefoot and pregnant?' The sarcasm was biting and painful.

'If I were to tell you the truth, the answer would be yes, but only to a successful Sicilian business man. He would expect my husband to give me a million dollar home in Halton Hills. In return, I would have lots of healthy bambinos.' Responding with her own self mockery decreased the tremor which threatened to derail her defiance. It still hurt that

17

her father refused to acknowledge the academic successes of her life.

'That's still your personal life. We are talking about nursing here. These girls today don't know one end of a bed pan from the other.' The disgust was back in Colleen's voice.

'There's more to nursing than bedpans. I certainly honed a lot of my practical skills when I studied midwifery in England, but new technology and education have enabled nurses to spend less time on practical unskilled tasks and more time on observation of patients, planning and continuity of care.'

'Too much time, if you ask me. Too much time is spent watching beeping machines instead of really seeing to patient care.'

'Oh Colleen that's not fair and you know it. We've had this argument before, one way or another and neither of us wins.' Rosanna's throat hurt. She had not shared her family story before tonight with her working partner. She loved her father deeply but it was clear that night work was taking its toll on her. 'Look Colleen, you and I combine our best skills and work for the benefit of everyone.'

'You are too smart for me Annie.'

'Not smarter, just different! You are the senior here.' she softened her tone, hoping to avoid escalating the ongoing discussion. 'I've learned a lot from you.'

'Sure, sure but it took me 30 plus years to get here. It took you less than ten years, Annie.'

'I worked hard to get here too.' Rosanna tried to keep her tone light but failed miserably.

'Ach, you're too touchy girl!'

The younger woman bent her head in frustration. Try as she might, she could not get past her partner's resentment of anything new in nursing. She knew that her Master's degree stood like a rock between them. Anger flared up in defiance then died out just as quickly. She genuinely liked the older woman and did not want to hurt Colleen. Rosanna had a tendency to let her flighty tongue run away without its common sense, intellectual partner. Quite often, she was unable to put the brakes on in time, to stop herself saying the wrong thing. She took a deep breath before continuing.

'I don't want to argue with you either. I left home to avoid just this type of endless argument, over similar issues. With my father, it's all about my continued single status. I refuse to replace him with you.'

Despite her wish to be cordial, the tone was sharp.

'Don't know what's got into you Annie. Maybe you do need to get married. Your father could be right.'

'He's not and quit calling me Annie. My name is Rosanna.'

Colleen knew she had gone too far. She subsided in her wooden chair. Since their desks faced forward, it was hard to ignore each other but they were both tired. The pile of paperwork seemed to grow in proportion to their fatigue. The change of shift loomed. The reports had to be completed.

Rosanna sighed and closed her eyes. She took another deep breath. *'Whoever hired me knew exactly what they were doing'* she thought indignantly. Colleen could be very difficult at times but most nights, Rosanna allowed things to pass in order to maintain unity. Too many shifts in a row seemed to have taken their toll.

'Why am I sitting here trying to soothe this poor lady's ego at five o'clock in the morning? Maybe she and Papa are right. I should be home in bed, curled up with a husband, while my two kids are sound asleep in their room.'

Not having a current boyfriend to fill in the face of the imaginary husband, she was dismayed to find that the partially masked face of Dr. Howard came unwanted into the picture of her make believe family. Still seething over his attitude towards her during their work on the little baby, she returned to the papers littered on her desk firmly quashing the scarecrow-like features from her consciousness.

∞

'Was it a bad night Rosanna?'

'No worse than usual. A couple of emergencies happened on pediatrics.' The dismissing shrug was designed to end any confidences. 'I've done seven nights in a row so I want to get out of here quickly. Colleen took the last call so she'll give you the final unit reports. Three staff reported sick. Two have been replaced by agency staff and Andrews will come in to work overtime today in peds. They had a pretty busy night and still have some touch and go patients.'

'Seven nights…I am so glad I don't have to do that night shift anymore. You always manage to find staff to work Rosanna.'

Despite stating clearly that she didn't want to prolong the morning hand over, Vanessa, the day shift supervisor continued to try to engage in conversation.

'When you come from a big family you learn how to be persuasive. Now, let's go through these reports.' A sweet smile took any sting out of her voice. Within minutes, Rosanna was on her way to the comfort of her downtown condominium.

Chapter 2

Rosanna had always been very careful with money, paying off her student loan in record time. She had purchased a one bedroom condominium using her savings and a small donation from her father to make the down payment. It was a perfect investment. The site was convenient to every major shopping and entertainment centre in the Greater Toronto Area. More importantly it was just a few minutes' walk from the hospital. On bad weather days, the transportation service was virtually door to door in seconds. Rosanna enjoyed the short walk in the evenings. Although she was most often going to work after dark, the city was not yet overrun with crime, as was often found in other metropolitan areas. Rarely did she feel unsafe. The main street was well lit and busy with pedestrians. At least one police station was close by. As a bonus, a late night coffee house, which served a passable espresso, was open.

After her long and busy night shifts, Rosanna would walk home, loving the early morning sunlight. She enjoyed the opportunity to purchase newly delivered produce at a small market store. The smell of fresh bread straight from the oven of a nearby bakery wafted past her nose and tempted an indulgence clearly designed to add pounds to her figure. Fatigue often helped her to avoid the pull of nature's staple food but on other days, the warm bread covered with melting butter could not be resisted.

She was much too tired to enjoy any of the offerings available. The stressful emergencies and the emotionally draining discussion with Colleen exacerbated her natural fatigue. The front doors of her condominium building beckoned and she entered them with a sigh of relief. After a brief ride in the unoccupied elevator, Rosanna was soon inserting her key into the lock.

As she let herself into the small foyer leading to a spacious living dining area, Rosanna reflected on the luck which allowed her to purchase the conveniently located unit, with a minimum of fuss and at a reasonable price. The previous owners, a young expectant couple, needing to move, were anxious to sell. Fully air-conditioned, the building contained all the modern conveniences including downtown underground parking, a fully equipped exercise room, a heated swimming pool with Jacuzzi and security services. The south facing condo offered an unrestricted view of the city including Lake Ontario which was clearly visible from the tenth floor. It was not an adequate space for a family but suited a single woman perfectly.

Rosanna purchased a large salmon coloured couch with pull-out capabilities in case of the occasional overnight visitor. A slightly darker matching chair complimented the casually elegant look. The combination porch/den contained a comfy lazy boy, a small study desk and chair. Several plants thrived under the morning sun. Next to the living room was an eat-in kitchenette. Rosanna chose not to have a formal dining room, using the allotted space to increase the total size of the living room. A guest powder room was located near the front entrance. Beyond the common living area and down a short hall, there was a large bedroom, complete with ensuite bathroom and walk in closet. The layout had generated a 'love at first sight' excitement in the normally conservative nurse. Careful decorating added the final touches, turning the area into a delightful home. This particular morning it felt like a haven.

Rosanna had three days off and planned to use them fully. The early June mornings seemed to explode into sunshine after a rainy, mediocre May. A good salary and security based on having a regular full time job enabled her to look forward to a summer in which she could explore the beauty and points of interest in the world class metropolitan city, if the good weather held. Night work often took a toll on nurses, but Rosanna had no young children whose needs she had to balance against the demands of a job. She only needed to take care of her own health and wellbeing. Rosanna hoped that somewhere down the road she would be able to secure a day job in the guise of a long hoped for promotion. The night supervisor's position had offered limited visibility but vast learning potential for the already highly educated nurse. When the time came to make a choice between work and family she would decide how to handle her future. For the present she was content.

Her immediate plan was to take a quick shower, sleep four to five hours and then make her way down to the central core of the city to do some shopping. As she darkened her room and prepared for sleep the mental list of things to do brought a smile to her face. The upcoming visit to a large bookstore would be the most enjoyable. There was a plethora of reading material covering every subject known to man. Some books she needed and could justify the purchase, but the joy of reading something new and exciting was the sole reason for her anticipation. As she thought about what genre she would purchase to fill her upcoming days, the combination blue and white colours of the bedroom melded and became clouds in a summer sky. Before long, even that faded to be replaced by a dreamless sleep.

∞

Seven hours later, Rosanna woke with a start, knowing that she slept well beyond the four hours. Furious with herself for sleeping so long, she rolled on to her back. *'I must have been more tired than I thought,'* she groaned, throwing the pillow at a bare wall. It was numbness in her arm which had forced her to wake up. Very soon it became a tingling mass of nerves. Shaking her hand to restore some feeling, she glanced at the clock surprised to see it was almost 4:30 in the afternoon. She muttered some nonsense to no one in particular, before jumping out of bed. A quick wash soon chased away the last of the sleep from her eyes.

Rosanna wouldn't postpone all her plans and simply put some of them on hold for another day. Not wanting to leave the house with an empty stomach, she prepared a light lunch. A veggie pasta salad with a tangy sauce helped to ease her disappointment about shopping but the bookstore was another matter. It would be open quite late. She was going there regardless. Dragging on a pair of navy slacks, white blouse, and low heeled shoes, she sailed out the door as if she had not a care in the world.

Rosanna had never been too conscious about her looks. Her average 5'3 inch height didn't add anything to her curvaceous figure but she felt that her lush Italian heritage tended to make her slightly more exotic and highly visible. Compared to the pristine Anglo-Saxon complexions which constituted the better part of Hamilton's less cosmopolitan make-up, she stood out like a sore thumb all through school. A wholly Latin shrug dismissed today what had been an adolescent concern. Her light olive skin and full lips were just who she was. At thirty-four, already mature beyond her years and a highly skilled professional, she was happy to acknowledge herself as simply doing her job. Many would have disagreed. Her large brown eyes and long lashes, beautifully set in a charming oval face, and classically Roman profile set her apart. Rosanna embodied all the qualities of a successful woman in the post modern feminist era.

∞

A brisk five minute walk took her to the entrance of the book store. She entered the cavernous warehouse style building with a deep intake of breath. For a book lover, it was like heaven. She didn't know where to begin but allowed her eyes to guide her feet. Rosanna picked out a couple of current non-fiction paperbacks, tapes of the latest movies to watch, a book about upcoming changes in natural therapies and few magazines.

Almost an hour later, the shopping basket on her arm was weighing her down. She made her way to the check out. There was no line up. She hesitated knowing that something was missing. Before committing herself to the check out, she retraced her steps, mentally searching her memory for the missing link. She soon remembered that an ICU emergency a couple of nights previously left her slightly puzzled. A cardiac tracing, which should have been clearly understood, made no sense. She wanted to review the protocols for reading ECG's but needed an up-to-date book. If she was to help the nurses, it was important to be cognizant of all situations. Her willingness to learn and to help made her a standout to all staff.

The medical section was located on the second floor, accessible by a mini escalator. The basket of books was getting exceedingly heavy. Rosanna quickly found the section where several recent publications in varying degrees of comprehension were lined up neatly on the shelf. Choosing a middle-of-the-road hardcover, which would keep her current, was enough. Sighing at the inevitability of Murphy's Law, the very book she wanted was on the bottom shelf. She rested the heavy basket on the floor.

Squatting, Rosanna balanced on the ball of her feet. She managed to insert two fingers around the spines of the book just as she was brushed ever so slightly from behind. She didn't shriek but landed with an ungainly thump on her bottom. Annoyed, she jumped up ready to do battle. It took a couple of spins before she found the culprit, head down on the other side of the book shelf. *'Darned if it wasn't that Dr. Howard again!'* she fumed inwardly. Her eyes fixed him with a steely glare. Rosanna long to vent out her frustrations from the early morning encounter, the oversleeping, and the ignominious fall, but her heart remembered his soft words to the little babe and she relented. Her lips parted on a deep calming breath, but the glare remained.

∞

Angus Howard was an intellectual gourmet. He spent most of his limited free time scouring book stores for medical research texts to enhance his work. He also sought and purchased antique books as a hobby. There was very little else of note in his life. He played squash four times a week with anyone willing to take him on. He rode his bicycle to work daily. Angus rarely socialized and was shunned by most of his colleagues. Life's subtleties also passed him by. He was straightforward, blunt to the point of rudeness when the situation warranted, but somehow found the wherewithal to be charming when he wanted money for his hospital research projects. He may have been surprised by what people thought of him, but generally he didn't care.

His head was bent over an enormous encyclopaedic book, which could, by the look of it, topple his thin frame with its weight. Few humans, however, could have withstood the glare directed at them and despite living in a cocoon of his own making, Angus did surface from time to time. He glanced up and was transfixed by two vaguely familiar golden brown eyes staring at him from the next aisle. The eyes were barely level with the top row of the shelf but he took off his reading glasses to be sure that he was not mistaken. It seemed he was indeed the object of the stare.

'My dear lady, do I know you?'

'I'm not an American Express commercial', she answered tartly.

'You should be!' he rejoined in a matter of fact tone, surprising even himself.

Rosanna tried not to be deterred by what might be construed as a compliment. She frowned, struggled to suppress a smile before giving up altogether. She could not find the words to be angry.

'You knocked me over a minute ago. I doubt that you did it on purpose but at the very least you could have apologized. I realize after this morning that you..that you....'

Rosanna was halted in mid sentence by his quick approach to her side of the book shelf. She was not intimidated by his extreme height. He looked so thin, she was sure she could best him in any fight. Anyway he looked more puzzled than aggressive.

'What does this morning have to do with me being rude? I don't think I've ever seen you before in my life, although there is something familiar about you.' He peered at her myopically, a deep frown marring his forehead.

Embarrassed and thinking she had made a mistake about him being the culprit, she opened her mouth to apologize unnecessarily when he stopped her.

'Do you work at the General?'

'Yes.'

'I see.'

Because he didn't say more she didn't know what he 'saw' and sent him a questioning glance.

'Your eyes and voice...' One hand held the book, the other was deep in his pocket. He swayed back and forth, as discerning eyes searched her face. Rosanna felt like bacteria in a Petri dish. The metaphor was silly. She tried to imagine herself doing the backstroke in the gel-like medium made solely for growing germs.

'Do I amuse you?'

Rosanna noted that the scarecrow pulled himself up slightly. She abandoned the scarecrow idea. Clearly, he possessed a brain. *'Maybe he's the tin woodsman,'* she thought, knitting her brows in turn.

Angus observed the mobility of her features. She wasn't laughing at him but she was clearly puzzled. The look was magnetic, felt different and yet familiar. It held him immobile.

Rosanna glanced up into his face, noting the full sculptured lips, the high prominent cheekbones, but got no further than his eyes. They were a startling colour of green, almost like lima beans. As the thought crossed her mind she smiled again, startling him with her perfect row of teeth, gold-brown eyes and dark feathery eyelashes. Rosanna was envious of those eyes with their unusual colour but Angus Howard was apoplectic. His indrawn breath had the sensation of a bullet, passing through his body, pulling his life force away. In a split second, when its energy returned, he sensed that he would never be the same person again.

For years, Angus had avoided most female contact, outside of his family. There had been relationships with a few girls through medical school. He indulged in an occasional fling, primarily to satiate his rather low sex drive but a few bad experiences left him wary of professional, high powered women. He was aware that most people thought he was gay. It wasn't true. He also refused to confirm or deny any such rumour by parading just any woman on his arm. His mind was devoted to his work, his body to fitness. Women and their fickle, demanding ways were abandoned.

'But this woman! Her smile!' He was filled with such an incredible feeling. Without thought, his mouth opened.

'Will you have dinner with me?'

'What?'

'Dinner…do you eat?'

'Don't be ridiculous. Of course I eat.'

'Then eat with me.'

'I don't understand. You knocked me over. Dinner isn't necessary. A simple *excuse me* would do.'

'Do you like to dance?'

'Yes, but…"

'Give me your address. I'll pick you up in ..ah..let's see…an hour and a half. Will that give you time?'

'For what?'

'To get ready, of course!'

At a loss for words and wondering when, if ever, she had said yes to the extraordinary proposal, Rosanna found herself giving the requested address but was totally unable to fathom why. Tucking the scrap of paper into his pocket, he continued to stare at her for a heart-stopping moment then added, 'I'm sorry I knocked you over. It wasn't intentional. 'Here' he said, picking up the basket, 'is this yours?'

She nodded, still too bemused by his quixotic overture. *'Mama would have a fit. She would be appalled that I could date someone so tall and skinny. She'd never approve.'* Rosanna thoughts filled the silence between them as they made their way to the check-out. She hurriedly paid for her purchases.

Dr. Howard didn't follow her out to the street but he did escort her as far as the door.

'Eight o'clock then.' His tone neither conveyed command nor request, just a statement of a given situation.

∞

An hour later Rosanna was still sitting on the couch, watching the clock, debating whether to go or not. The telephone jangled sharply, frightening her in the stillness of the apartment. She was almost afraid to pick it up.

'Miss Amadeo?'

'Yes speaking."

She recognized the tentative, high-pitched voice of Carol Wiseman, the evening supervisor.

'Ah, Rosanna...It's Carol. Lacey has called in sick tonight. Do you think... you can work?'

Rosanna really didn't want to work. Days off were very precious, but she also knew that they would have a difficult time finding senior staff who were familiar with the night routine. It would be a perfectly legitimate excuse to cancel her 'date' with Dr. Howard.

Her thoughts created a long hesitation.

'Do you have plans for tonight?'

"....Er... yes I do.... sort of."

The opportunity to say no was lost without looking foolish to her colleague. That wouldn't really matter. She knew

Carol would be happy just to settle things as quickly as possible.

Rosanna looked deep into her consciousness. She saw him in her mind's eye. He hadn't really begged her to go out. Demanded? No, 'expected' was the word she sought, but underneath his bony face, he seemed almost earnest, boyish. The look melted something inside of her.

'I really can't Carol. I'm sorry"

'It's okay Rosanna. I know it's Friday night. Anyway, Mrs. Tilsma said she'd come in if there was no one else. G'night, have a good time.'

Rosanna laughed after hanging up. *'Colleen will not have a good time tonight. The Dragon and the Bear, working together. … it should be interesting,'* she thought with a silly giggle. It was well known that the semi-retired Marte Tilsma brooked no nonsense. Even the usually aggressive Colleen quaked when the real old school nurse marched down the halls breathing pure fire on sleepy nurses. She spent too long contemplating the endless possibilities without remembering that she had committed herself, mentally at least, to the date.

'Oh no!' she moaned, looking at the clock. It was already 7:40.

Rosanna had a quick wash but wasted a minutes at the closet deciding between a red or blue dress for the evening. She chose the blue, thinking that it looked less provocative and stylish in case he decided on some place very simple to eat. Working faster than usual she was just about putting the finishing touches to her make-up when the intercom buzzed, dead on eight o'clock.

∞

So far, Rosanna had seen Dr. Howard perform a fairly common but dangerous procedure. He was careful, quick and precise. She should have expected him to be on time. Her hand trembled only slightly as the lipstick she had finished applying slipped easily into its case. Rosanna didn't hurry to the door, but kept her hand steady on the knob for support. She would not invite him up. It was too soon and the setting of her apartment might create an intimacy she was far from feeling.

'I'll be right down' she sang nervously into the speaker of the intercom, hating herself for the slight tell-tale tremor in her voice.

'I'm going out with a perfect stranger. I have no idea why. I must be impazza!' Shaking her head to dispel the 'craziness', she picked up her bag and opened the door, pushing all misgivings to the back of her mind. *'He seemed harmless enough'* she thought bolstering her own sagging confidence. *'At least I'll get a free meal out of it.'*

Only once during the ride down from the tenth floor did Rosanna contemplate turning back. Some sense of caution, deep inside, at the core of her common sense, felt compelled to push the stop button. She knew he would be downstairs in the foyer, able to track the movement of the elevator. Possibly, he would not be discerning enough to know if the car stopped mid ride. She could get off and take the other elevator returning to the 10th floor without seeing him at all. Rosanna knew her thoughts were unworthy, but fear of an unknown circumstance flickered along nerve endings, sending a clear signal that, if she continued, her life would never be the same again. Fate and free will warred within her. In a heartbeat, fate had taken over. The elevator landed on the ground floor with a soft whirr, ending any thought of retreat.

Chapter 3

Angus was enjoying the last of his strawberry cheesecake. He also kept a covert eye on the equally delicious looking woman seated opposite him. He was remembering the delightful vision, which met his eyes, as she walked off the elevator, looking every inch a Goddess. He shook his head slightly, unable to find the words to describe what he saw.

The blue dress she chose for the evening, fit like a glove over her rounded hips. The split at the back gave a tantalizing glimpse of shapely thighs. She wore high heels which accentuated her well formed calves and slim ankles. He had never seen anyone walk in shoes like that. She did it with grace and style. Glancing at her now, he could see a small expanse of neck and shoulder visible at the collar of her dress. The quaint top belied the sensuous skirt. Her shoulder length hair shone blue-black in the subdued lighting of the restaurant.

Angus decided to dine at the Keg Mansion, preferring the more secluded upstairs. He ate out often and invariably alone, gravitating to large public places like this where he blended in and became just another anonymous diner. It was his wish to remain undisturbed. His own thoughts, filled with the needs of his job that required hours of problem solving, satisfied him more than time wasted on idle chatter.

'She didn't talk much either,' he thought. Her raven hair and lush beauty seemed at variance with a controlled demeanour, manifesting as tension in her body. She appeared to hold herself in check, almost as if she were afraid. *'Why should she have come out with me anyway? We are virtually strangers.'* There was little comfort in his analysis but something inside was driving his actions. Allowing irrational feelings, to override his normal taciturn nature, was a surprise.

Angus wasn't adept at small talk, a practice he had lost through disuse. Consequently, a disquieting silence punctuated bouts of desultory conversation during the meal. Both had tucked into the mouth watering steak and mushroom dinner, the specialty of the house. Rosanna enjoyed a glass of red wine. Angus, who didn't drink, had sparkling water. They were almost finished dessert before Angus realized that he couldn't put a first name to the woman he had been admiring throughout the meal. When he asked for her address at the store, that's all she gave him.

'What's your first name?' he blurted out embarrassed by his teenage awkwardness.

'Rosanna. What's yours?'

'Angus' he replied. She smiled widely, that perfect row of beautifully shaped teeth, clearly visible and irresistible. His embarrassment disappeared. He stared at the hand stretched across the table. It was her right hand and he captured it in his left, before realizing that she meant to shake hands formalizing their belated self introductions. It gave him the opportunity to study the pink tips, devoid of polish. The creamy soft, olive skin, felt like silk to his touch, stirring some long suppressed emotions within him.

'Are you Spanish or Italian heritage?' he added releasing her hand reluctantly.

'Italian.'

'From Toronto?'

'No Hamilton…and you?'

'Toronto.' He didn't expand on his heritage.

They fell silent again, finishing what remained of their dessert.

'Coffee?'

'No thank you. I would like a cappuccino though.'

Angus liked her manners. Clearly, she had an independent mind.

'Do you have any preference where we go dancing? I don't want to appear too boastful but I'm pretty good at most types of music, with the exception of the current hard rock songs.'

Surprised that the evening was to continue, Rosanna replied 'no, you choose. Anything is fine with me.'

She spoke softly, a smile on her face. He was more than a bit uncomfortable. '*Was she enjoying herself?*', he wondered. '*I seem to be doing this all wrong. I haven't dated in nearly two years and the last time was a complete disaster*'. Annoyance marred the smooth brow as he remembered the colleague at a conference who questioned his manhood when he refused to join her in bed. She had been attractive but too heavily made up. Most of the time, she talked like a computer printout. His refusal turned her into a venomous virago spouting such obscenities that he quickly backed off, convinced that nice women didn't exist.

Rosanna saw the frown and worried that she had done something. 'Is anything wrong?' she asked tilting her head to one side.

'No, I was just wondering….if I...uh …turned off the stove. The improvisation was clearly a lie but she let it go and he rushed on before she could say anything to end the evening prematurely. 'There's a big band playing at the Pavilion. Would that interest you?'

'I'd love to try.'

Her quiet willingness warmed his spirit. He hoped she would be a good dancer. '*She must be,*' he thought wistfully, '*if the way she walked was any indication*'.

They didn't linger over the remnants of their meal. Their minds were already made up and by tacit agreement they both looked forward to extending the evening. Angus discreetly settled the bill before they headed out to the car.

∞

Rosanna was feeling a few butterflies. The dinner had gone fairly well, but he hadn't talked much. The drive from her apartment to the restaurant had been too short for much of an exchange. It was impossible to engage in any meaningful conversation while negotiating busy downtown traffic.

Angus seemed placid, not at all as abrasive as he had been at work. Unlike many modern men, he afforded her every courtesy, assisting her in and out of the car, guiding her up the stairs to their table.

The dates usually arranged by her brother Dominic, with her father's approval, were often self centered men, intent on having an old fashioned wife they could control. Rosanna was never certain why Dominic thought she needed protection. Angus was different. He seemed to care about her needs, moving beyond his own to make her comfortable.

As they made their way through the parking lot, Rosanna considered that she and Angus didn't appear to have much else in common. She wondered what the rest of the evening would bring. It was nearly ten o'clock. Rosanna decided that if things didn't work out she would plead fatigue. He wasn't to know that she had slept all day.

'You know….' He hesitated while making a left turn onto the main thoroughfare. Once driving south towards the lake he continued. 'After I left you this afternoon, I wasn't at all sure that you would come tonight.' The words were accompanied by a quick glance at her profile. He was entranced again by the lovely bow shaped mouth which did little things to his insides when she smiled.

'I wasn't sure myself,' she replied honestly, sensing a need to be frank.

'Why did you?'

'I said I would, or at least, I implied that I would.'

'Thank you Rosanna.'

It was her turn to glance at him. From the tight angle of

the car, the fey quality of his thin face was less marked. The long nose stood out starkly with the angular jaw line adding a perfect balance. *'His eyes are what give him the feminine look.. What an unusual colour they are! The lashes are so long'* she thought on a sigh, envious again of how Mother Nature dispenses coveted attributes.

She stared for so long that he glanced back at her, a slightly bewildered look on his face. To cover her confusion, she rushed on.

'They did call me to come in tonight but somehow I just couldn't.' Rosanna laughed nervously but the sounds sent his insides into frenzy. The spacious wine coloured jaguar had suddenly become too confining and he shifted trying to ease an unexpected ache in his groin.

'May I ask why you are laughing?' He sounded curious and a little offended.

Rosanna hurried on to reassure him. 'I was just thinking about Colleen MacGregor. She will be working with Marte Tilsma tonight.' Rosanna didn't want to gossip and added no embellishment. If he worked at the General he would be aware of the 'dragon lady' Marte and her reputation.

'Do you know Colleen MacGregor?' he demanded, dismissing Miss Tilsma from the conversation.

'Of course I do. We work together on nights.'

'Are you Annie?' he asked, clearly surprised at the reply she had given.

'No! I am Rosanna. I know Colleen calls me that all the time. But, how did you know?'

42

'She's my aunt, my mother's sister!'

'You mean..... **you** are Gussie?!' Rosanna was incredulous.

'I am afraid so' he replied wryly. 'My aunt has a propensity for choosing her own names for people and that's mine. It can be quite annoying.'

'*No kidding!*' Rosanna thought, but kept the comment to herself. She was digesting the unexpected information. Angus continued trying to fill the breech which her silence created.

'I try to stay out of her way at work. The hospital is large but she is high profile among the nurses and they love to gossip, so I call her Ms. MacGregor and she calls me Dr. Howard. '

Rosanna was still unable to make any comment about this new knowledge. Colleen didn't talk much about her personal life, but time and the isolation of night work loosened tongues. Over the past year, references to 'Gussie' and his research program cropped up often. Rosanna had shown appropriate though half-hearted interest murmuring assent or dissent when necessary. One fact was very clear however. 'Gussie' was the apple of her eye. Rosanna wondered how old he was. Colleen made him seem as if he were fresh out of college. He looked much older she conceded. Another thought popped into her head.

'Is there a real Annie?' she demanded. 'I don't know why Colleen insists on calling me by that name.'

Angus didn't look thoughtful or puzzled. To her surprise, he laughed loudly, throwing back his head as the deep sound rumbled around the car. Glancing at her quickly he noted, 'Yes! That's it, of course. You do look like her.'

He didn't seem in any hurry to answer her question. *'He's just like his Aunt,'* she thought crossly. There was no time to repeat the question however. The car was gliding smoothly into the parking lot near a beautiful gothic looking structure. The edifice, disused for years, was once a lake side bathing Pavilion earlier in the last century. Through loving hands, it had been carefully restored and returned to life.

Known as Sunnyside, it was now Toronto's own beach playground. The park covered several acres along the shoreline of Lake Ontario. The area remained a popular gathering place almost every day of the week. Families, couples and all manner of young people came for picnics, parties or just strolling along the boardwalk. There were playgrounds, swimming pools, food kiosks, fishing wharves, a yacht club and the old Pavilion where dancing under the stars was making a comeback.

As they entered between the large white columns at the front portico, the lively brass sound of a big band was belting out popular tunes reminiscent of the Glen Miller era.

'I hope we can find a table. This place is getting more and more crowded every year,' Angus mumbled, looking around.

'Do you come here often?' Rosanna inquired in a stilted manner. She was still peeved that he had not satisfied her curiosity. There was something significant in the name. She wanted to know why Colleen elected to call her Annie.

'If Colleen doesn't want to tell you why she calls you Annie, I certainly can't,' he replied not answering either question.

He looked directly at her. She could detect a mischievous glint in his eye and relented gracefully.

'I am going to keep on asking though.'

'No harm in that.'

Angus guided her smoothly into the dancing area. The hand at the small of her back was firm, unconsciously encouraging her to relax and allow him to take care of everything. For an independent minded woman, the release was enlightening. Rosanna rarely let down her guard but acknowledged to herself that she felt safe rather than controlled. It was an odd sensation and one she would analyze later. Instead, she chose to give herself up to the moment.

There was a fair sized crowd but they were lucky to find a small table for two, tucked away in a far corner of the large room near the band. Conversation was impossible over the sound of the brass and woodwind section. They tacitly agreed to just sit and listen, enjoying the colourful swirl of dancers encircling the room.

Several French doors led out onto a terrace which overlooked the lake, ghostly now with barely a crescent moon in the sky. Angus motioned an inquiry about drinks. Rosanna nodded, mouthing for a glass of wine.

He excused himself and headed towards the bar giving her an opportunity to observe his gait. It was almost like a sailor's roll, fluid and unhurried. '*He has big feet*' she noted, giggling stupidly with sudden nervousness. The dark suit that he wore fit surprisingly well over his meager frame. The golden blond hair, slicked down firmly two hours ago, now began to tumble over one eye. It wasn't long, nor cut in any particular shape but seemed healthy and very full for a man past the first bloom of youth.

Twenty minutes later, relaxed and warmed by the atmosphere, they made their way onto the dance floor. The band was playing a set of slower tunes. Starting out at a more sedate pace allowed them to make natural adjustments to each other's style. Very little awkwardness seemed to mar their initial movements together.

∞

Rosanna didn't know where time went. Song after song played on. She and Angus were still moving around the floor with ease. He wasn't even winded after several energetic tunes. *'He's a superb dancer'* she thought dreamily, hopeful that she had held her own.

They were back in each other's arms as the pace slowed once more, but this time he held her closely, his chin resting on her head, her hand cupped at his shoulder, their thighs touching intimately. They moved so well that Rosanna felt as if she were standing on his toes, light as a feather, supported by his arms, and floating through the air.

'Are you tired?' he whispered softly when she sighed in his arms.

'A little, but I don't want to stop…unless you do?' She looked up then. Her last words were not a question but a statement to him that said she was content.

He didn't want to stop now or ever. She felt like gossamer, a wrapped flower, all softness, smelling like a spring day, delicate yet firm. For the second time that evening Angus felt his senses stir. He would be embarrassed if she noticed so he loosened his hold slightly to look at her again.

'I'm not tired but I haven't forgotten that you worked last night. It's almost one,' he said glancing at a large wall clock. 'We can always do this again if you like.'

'I like…' she breathed out on a sigh, before allowing him to lead her back to the table for her purse.

Each of them made a trip to the facilities on the way out. Rosanna went for the usual reasons but Angus desperately needed to splash his face with cold water. As she had spoken those last words, her breath slid softly into the space between his shirt buttons arousing him to the point of near suffocation. The warmth of it tingled the hairs on his chest; something he never even guessed could be erotic.

'I thought I had better control. My God! What must she think of me?' he berated his reflection in the bathroom mirror… *'panting after her like a stallion in heat'.* The comparison was crude and not worthy of his usual ascetic nature. He was a scientist, an intellectual, but since his encounter with Rosanna, in the book store, his nature seemed to have undergone profound changes. The stallion imagery would not subside, no matter how hard he tried.

Rosanna was waiting for him when he finally emerged from the men's room. She had her eyes closed and was leaning against a white pillar swaying back and forth to the muted sounds coming from inside. He stood watching her for some moments, the rise and fall of her breasts, the swaying of her hips, the slight bobbing of her head in perfect time with the music. Angus wanted her back in his arms. He wanted her in his bed. He wanted her naked and doing all of those things under his body.

Angus nearly choked on the frankly sexual images. Whatever resolve the scientist in him made, the lover, aching for release, overruled. *'I've got to get her home before I lose my mind,'* he decided, truly frightened by his feelings. *'I just won't see her anymore. That's it!'*

Angus approached Rosanna cautiously. He elected to adopt a cold and withdrawn manner. The scientist had the upper hand, if only temporarily.

∞

Sitting in the comfortable car on the drive home, Rosanna felt completely relaxed. Angus seemed to withdraw a little when he met her at the pavilion entrance. *'He was probably tired too,'* she concluded. After all, he had also been up for most of the night. She had no idea why there had been a subtle change in his mood and didn't really care at that moment. She only knew that she hadn't felt this soothed in years.

Rosanna had no awareness of arriving back at the condominium. During the drive home, she had drifted off to sleep, giving lie to her words about not being tired. She awoke to the sound of her name, whispered sweetly in her ear.

'Rosanna, you're home. I'll escort you to your door.'

'No need. I can find my way.'

'That's a lie. You are more than half asleep.'

'I think I was completely asleep,' she mumbled.

Graciously accepting her limitations, she allowed him to

assist her to the door. They were halted in the main foyer by a deep voice.

'You can't park there all night sir.'

'Why would you assume that I intend to park there all night?'

The beefy looking security guard had appeared out of nowhere. His words were not aggressive. The warning was given in a dutiful manner but Angus would have given anything to stay with her. Guilt made him angrier than he needed to be.

'He's just seeing me to the door, Alex.'

'OK, g'nite Miss'

'Was I really awful?' Angus asked boyishly. They were speeding up in the elevator, his cold withdrawn attitude long forgotten, as he watched her sleep in the car.

'Yes you were. Poor Alex was just looking out for my best interests and the safety of your car. You could get towed you know.'

'You're not angry with me?' he asked softly as the elevator doors opened.

Rosanna's condo was only two doors away. She held her reply until she reached her door and located her keys.

'No Angus. After such a wonderful evening that, I might add, I never expected, I'd have a hard time being angry with anyone, least of all you.' It was a pretty speech. She wanted him to kiss her. She knew that he had been aroused earlier and felt flattered considering his less than aggressive masculinity. He seemed too much of a gentleman to take advantage anyway. She hoped that she communicated openness with her words.

'Rosanna I…'

'Come in for a few minutes' she invited, opening the door.

'I don't think I should' he averred, but followed her regardless. She stopped and turned around to question his refusal not realizing that he was so close behind her.

'Why n…?' She ran into him full force.

His arms came around her to steady them both. They stared at each other wordlessly. Her lips parted on a sigh and he, wanting her so desperately, couldn't resist. The kiss was short. There was no seeking or deepening. She was content to feel the fullness of his body so close, to thread her fingers in his hair. He was afraid and held back. Neither was sure, each was merely taking the measure of the other.

Angus broke away reluctantly. He was breathing heavily. Placing his hands on her shoulders he stared, for a heart stopping moment, holding her lovely, sleepy eyes, with his own.

'Spend the day with me tomorrow?'

'Yes.'

'I'll pick you up at nine. Good night Rosanna.'

He was gone, leaving her standing at the door, bemused and too full of sensual delight to say more.

Eventually she made her way down the short corridor to her bedroom. Despite dancing for hours, in high heeled shoes, her footsteps were light. Arms wrapped around her body trying to recreate the feeling of being held by him. It was the first time in years that she had gone out with a man other than a 'respectable Italian' properly chosen by her family.

It's only one date, she admitted soothing her conscience. She kicked off the high heels and sat down. In that moment, she could feel the unaccustomed exercise. Rosanna massaged the sore muscles in her feet and legs. She refused to feel guilty about the evening, or her date. *'I'll spend the day with him tomorrow and go home on Sunday,'* she bargained inwardly, hoping that at least one day in Hamilton would appease her family. Satisfied with her decision, Rosanna hurriedly got ready for bed. Neither sleep nor sweet dreams were long in coming.

Chapter 4

Unknown to Rosanna, Saturday morning promised to be a sunny beautiful day. She had been able to sleep deeply, contentment relaxing her body for the first part of the night. Eventually she became fitful, dreaming of a tense and nerve racking life in the forest. A big black bear stole her food and ran off. She gave chase only to watch the bear turn into a much faster and more cunning fox. She was irritable when the alarm sounded at 7:30 am. *'I just hate the adjustment from night to day when I'm not working,'* she moaned into her best friend, the pillow, and promptly went back to sleep.

An insistent buzzing sound soon punctured her dreamy bubble and she jumped up startled to find that it was 9:05. *Oh my God! Angus!,* she wailed in consternation before stumbling out of bed and running down the hall. A quick press on the intercom soon stopped the nagging summons.

'Hello…Hello'

'It's Angus. Did I wake you?'

'Yes you did. Come on up anyway. It won't take me long to get ready.'

Rosanna ran to the bathroom to brush her teeth and splash water on her face. She gave little thought to her appearance. Angus had behaved like a perfect gentleman the previous evening. She felt quite safe greeting him in her pajamas. He could always have a cup of coffee while she finished dressing. The creamy silk two-piece was modest enough. Regardless of that, Rosanna had no idea where her robe was, gave up trying to remember and ran back down the hall to open the door with as much decorum as she could muster.

'Good morning Angus. I am really sorry...I ...was.... was...'

Rosanna got no further. The sleep had left her. She looked up into his face to complete the sentence but was halted by a different looking man from the one she dated last night. The body, which appeared so thin, was nothing of the kind. In three quarter length shorts, the long legs, covered by a fine golden down were pure sinewy muscle.

'How could I ever have thought him skinny?' she queried mentally, staring stupidly at the limbs before her. Her eyes fell to the white socks tucked in a pair of comfortable looking runners. Rosanna didn't know if she wanted to make the trip up the rest of his body again. The only way to know for sure if he was the same man would be to see his eyes but that meant a quick observation of lightly tanned arms encased in furry platinum down this time. The Polo shirt surely matched his unusual eyes, the collar wrapping itself around the firm cords in his neck.

Rosanna swallowed hard but continued upwards, missing the eyes altogether before settling her gaze on the blond hair, unruly today and falling over his forehead giving him a boyish air. He smelled clean, wholesome and looked the same.

'May I come in or have you gone back to sleep?'

'Huh?'

'Sleeping?'

'I'm sorry Angus. You look so different from last night. I… uh…. wasn't sure if you were the same person.'

'You look very different today too. And, I might add, very appealing in that white silky thing.'

Rosanna smiled shyly, accepting his compliment with an uncharacteristic blush.

'Don't tease me please.'

'If it doesn't please you, I won't', he offered with a laugh.

She motioned for him to come in, admiring his trim body as he moved forward into the small foyer of the condo. Her mind refused to dwell on what happened the last time they were in the same spot.

Rosanna wasn't sure how to proceed but knew what she needed most of all.

'Angus, can you make some coffee?'

'Can I or would I?' he asked tilting his head to one side in an endearing way.

'OK, would you?' she corrected with a slight frown thinking it was too early in the day for a grammar lesson.

Angus hesitated, looking embarrassed. Rosanna suddenly felt uncomfortable. She didn't really know this man very well. Didn't know him at all, in fact, and yet she felt so comfortable with him, that asking a simple every day task shouldn't make either of them so awkward. Rosanna felt like a very poor hostess but really all she wanted to do was get washed and dressed. She hated being unprepared for the date. She was about to apologize when Angus spoke up running his hand through the unruly hay stack on top of his head.

'The fact is that I am not…very good in the kitchen. I would make coffee, if I could.'

'You can't cook?' Rosanna drew out every word in disbelief. 'Not even boil water?' she prompted when he shook his head wryly.

'Where do you eat?' Rosanna's eyes were wide with incredulity, her hands moving in a wholly Italian way.

'At work or out! There's ample culinary services around Toronto and if all else fails, there's... Mom.'

Angus showed little remorse for his inability to provide the basic necessities for himself. Rosanna stood at the entrance to the kitchenette looking up at him. She was angry about waking up late, disturbed physically by this sexy oaf who looked better than he had a right to, and dying for a cup of decent coffee to stop a world that didn't make sense to her night oriented body. In vain she tried to tell him in measured words what to do but gave up when he just stared blankly at the coffee maker.

"I refuse to drink instant. Go and sit down' she commanded firmly, 'I'll do it myself'.

Angus headed for the living room. He heard a torrent of Italian streaming out of the kitchen while doors, cups, and pots were banged noisily. He wasn't worried. She had given him a look at the door, which activated senses he thought were long dead within him. Her attitude wasn't sexual in nature yet the eyes and body language conveyed a sense of awareness of him as a man. Her behaviour only validated his impressions. He hadn't studied human development for nothing. *'I only have trouble with myself,'* he decided, not caring to do any deep self analysis. Ignoring an obvious need for some self scrutiny, he walked calmly towards a well stocked book shelf which covered half of the living room wall.

He closed his mind to the words pouring from the kitchen and tried to pick-up some clue to her personality by the carefully laid out library. He could see that she loved literature as well as poetry, and modern biographies. She was also neat, and well organized, but then her manner and dress had already told him that. Clearly she was an avid and eclectic reader, judging by the variety of books on the shelves. There was, however, a very small section that contained four very old hardcover books. The antique collector bent over and peered at the titles before carefully removing a much handled tome.

"Before I Sleep" - Dr. Tom Dooley. Interesting!' he mused quietly, opening the pages very carefully.

'I wanted to join the humanitarian team he founded when I first graduated.'

Angus hadn't known she was watching him. He looked up to find her standing in the archway of the kitchen, smiling. With his full attention directed at her, Rosanna continued.

'A grateful patient gave me that book as inspiration. If you want to read it you'll have to do it here' she warned softly, liking the gentle way he handled her well-loved treasures.

'No. It wouldn't be necessary. I have a paperback copy. I also have the books he wrote, if you want to read the others.'

She waited a moment then asked quietly, 'do you like books?'.

'You could say that. My father, who is a true blue Scotsman by nature and birth has, to his chagrin, deep roots in northern England. As a constant and sometimes painful reminder of his family's true origins, he was forced to teach English literature to disinterested and insensitive high school students. Keep that in mind, when you come to my place. You'll be pleasantly surprised, I hope.'

'When?'

'Yes.'

'Not if you can't feed me.' There was no rebuke in her voice, just a gentle teasing. Her temper dissipated while she vented pent up frustration in the kitchen

'Did you eat this morning?' she asked before he could make any further excuses for his lack of culinary skills.

'I left at seven to play squash, then came right here.'

'Did you or didn't you?' she persisted feeling like a dentist with a difficult tooth.

'No.'

Taking a calming breath, she counted to ten in her mind. 'Would you like some scrambled eggs, sausages, toast, and juice to go with the coffee?'

'Yes please.'

Rosanna laughed, exasperated by this man who seemed to make her feel like a mother at her wit's end. She didn't know whether to slap or hug him. The *naughty boy* look was back in place and quite irresistible.

'Sit down and wait. I'll call you when it's ready.'

Angus was only too glad to sit. He used the book he was holding to hide what was becoming an embarrassment. Every time she smiled he felt something inside respond. It was getting to be a real problem, but he knew that he would not want to be anywhere else right now.

When he had recovered sufficiently, his nose became aware of a tantalizing aroma emanating from the kitchen. He wanted to seek the source but dared not risk going in. He would have to be insane. Subsiding meekly on the couch, Angus forced his mind to enjoy the visual feast which the book provided. The scientist had no strength against Rosanna and a plate of delicious smelling food.

'You're a marvel. I never knew scrambled eggs could taste so good,' Angus mumbled taking another piece of toast.

The fluffy eggs flavored with rosemary and onions were not a testament to her best culinary skills but she knew it would taste delicious to someone who couldn't cook.

'You eat out too much. It's not good for you' Rosanna admonished, ignoring the compliment.

'I suppose.' He looked only mildly contrite.

'You've heard all that before eh?'

'Oh yes, and often too.'

Rosanna didn't probe. She was curious about who could be watching his diet but resisted the impulse to ask that question and said instead , ' *I have no precious time at all to spend; Nor services to do, till you require, so...uh...*would you know how to wash dishes?'

'You quote Shakespeare. I am surprised,' he said, ignoring her question.

Rosanna raised her eyebrows. 'My father is a carpenter. He can tell you the measurement of a piece of wood, just by looking at it. My mother can sew a dress from one picture in a book and cook without a measuring cup. My older brother is an architect. Math is in our blood. The only way I could get a moment to draw attention to myself, was to quote Shakespeare's bite. No one could ever understand me but they paid attention.' She ended with a shrug of her shoulders.

Angus looked astonished by the surprising litany of information. He laughed loudly in response, throwing his head back, just as he had the previous night in the car. The column of his neck was tightened and muscular, though not thick. She longed to plant a kiss in the soft hollow under his Adam's apple and feel the vibration of his laughter through her lips. Thought of the impulsive act and the accompanying flare of desire surprised her. To cover up her discomfort she adopted an air of efficiency.

'I have to shower and change. It's nearly eleven o'clock. If I sit here much longer we'll never get away' she explained into his smiling face. His responsive look told her that he wouldn't mind.

Tearing his eyes from the seductive pull of her golden brown ones, he belatedly agreed to wash up. 'We do a lot of that in the lab. I'll be very careful too.' he promised sincerely.

'You'd better,' she admonished.

Rosanna got up from her chair breaking the intimacy created by the small table in the kitchenette and promptly stubbed her still bare toe. She leaned over the table to rub the smarting digit and found Angus' absorbing gaze centred on the pair of bobbing breasts only inches from his face. He nearly choked on the last of his coffee. Nothing was said. Their heightened awareness of each other was making itself felt. Ignoring the painful toe, she limped from the kitchenette.

Rosanna hurriedly dressed in a khaki coloured shorts set with a scooped neck jungle-pattern blouse under the short-sleeved jacket. Less than an hour later, they left the apartment. Rosanna said little but she was not as uncomfortable, as she had been the night before, by the long silences between them. She now knew him as Colleen's nephew. A year of information about his research enabled her to see him as someone other than a slightly off-beat doctor, with pretty eyes, who didn't know how to talk. She did not even care to examine any long term repercussions of seeing him. She enjoyed his quiet company, his good manners, and even his ability to bring out different sides of her nature.

At the front entrance to her building, he showed more

consideration for her comfort and well being. 'I didn't bring my car, Rosanna. Would you prefer to take a taxi?'

'Not really. To be honest, I haven't had much time to explore Toronto since I've been here. If you know the city perhaps you could give me a mini tour as we go along.'

'It would be my pleasure.' Crossing the thoroughfare at the lights, Angus changed his tone. 'Here we have our infamous transportation system,' he announced pointing out the obvious. 'I think this is the only city in the world where the local transit service can provide nearly every type of vehicle known to man.'

Laughing at his tour guide monotone they boarded the electrically powered streetcar in the familiar red and yellow colours. Taking his 'job' seriously Angus continued explaining the various points of interest along the busy route.

'On your left you'll see one of Toronto's oldest hospitals. Built in 1895, it was an early training school for both nurses and doctors. The close affiliation with the University of Toronto, which you will see on your right, continues to provide support for training and programs'. 'Don't blink,' he warned as the streetcar continued smoothly along its tracks 'or you'll miss our provincial Parliament buildings with its usual group of protesters dotting the well-kept lawns.'

'Please stop Angus' Rosanna pleaded laughing very hard. When she could talk she looked him in the eye. 'We could have taken a different route than the one I use every day, you know.'

'We could have, Rosanna, but then I would have been forced to talk with some degree of knowledge and expertise, which

I sadly lack. Another day we can really explore Toronto together with a professional. It has given me far more pleasure to make you laugh.'

'Angus I.....'

She was unable to say more. His beautiful eyes were mesmerizing. The moment was interrupted by the sound of the driver calling out the name of their transfer point.

Angus had indicated that there would be a long walk from the streetcar terminal. Rosanna wore low heeled espadrilles which were very comfortable. Angus was also suitably shod, but his long strides ate up the distance very quickly and she had some difficulty keeping pace with him. She was breathless and more than a little annoyed when they finally reached the ticket booth. To make things worse, Angus was barely winded.

'Do you always move so fast?'

'Sorry Rosanna, habit I guess.' His apologetic smile was warming. Rosanna felt another upsurge of the physical awareness that she had experienced earlier.

'Where would you like to go first?' he asked gently admiring her flushed cheeks and bright eyes, but failing to attribute them to anything except good health.

'Let's just walk around and explore, but very slowly, ok.?'

Angus chuckled before apologizing again. Taking her hand firmly, they set off at a very sedate pace. The path led to the children's village where young people of all sizes, shapes, and colours romped freely under the watchful eyes of exhausted parents.

'Makes me wish I was young again' Rosanna commented wistfully.

'Have you never been here before?'

'No, we lived in Hamilton, so my parents wouldn't have been able to plan a trip out of the city. My father worked so hard during the week that Sundays were quiet religious days at home.'

'Every generation has their own fun, Rosanna, in their own way.'

'I know, Angus. I'm not really resentful. My parents did the best they could. Family was very important to us so we made the most of birthdays, religious holidays, and ceremonies as they came along. I just hope this generation appreciates the wonder of a technological age that can support this type of activity.'

'Look around' he said waving his long arm in front of them. 'Have you ever seen a happier, healthier bunch of kids?'

'To be honest.....no,' she admitted.

'There's something else you should see.' he added dragging her reluctantly to an area that was enclosed and clearly marked 'FOR CHILDREN ONLY'. 'Look inside. Do you see anything modern or hi-tech?'

She had to admit that she didn't. The kids seem to be making their own fun out of ropes, rubber tires, and plastic shapes which could be anything. Nothing was defined except in the imagination of each child.

'It's all so simple, isn't it?'

'Yes it is simple and not very different from the games that we used to invent as kids.'

She felt Angus staring at her averted face. Her own gaze was absorbed by the mass of miniature humanity tumbling around beyond the mesh wire fence.

Rosanna smiled wistfully at the scene. Deep in the recesses of her mind she conjured up pictures of her own youthful days. They weren't all happy and carefree, though. An involuntary shadow of some remembered pain crossed her features. Before it could take root she felt Angus touch her arm.

'Let's go, Rosanna. There's a lot more to see.'

She turned to face him then, her eyes suspiciously moist. Everything faded from sight and sound at that moment. She had been a little girl again. As the moist golden brown encountered the uniquely green eyes of the man watching her tenderly, the little girl faded to be replaced by a woman vulnerable physically to the proximity of a man she barely knew. Every part of her body came alive.

Despite a tight grip on the fence, she felt herself straining towards the hand outstretched before her. The action was not meant to convey agreement to his request but an entreaty to caress her tension filled body and soothe the turmoil she refused to acknowledge as desire.

She saw Angus raise his eyebrows in a silent query. Before she could open her mouth to put words to something she didn't understand, Angus' head turned sharply, then disappeared from view. It took a second for Rosanna to realize that he was on his knees, speaking softly to a sobbing child of four or five years old, trying to encourage her to describe a 'mommy ' who seemed to be lost.

'I know a place where lost mommies can go' Angus reassured gently. 'If you give me your hand we'll walk over there together. My friend and I were lost too. My name is Angus. What's yours?'

The little blond head nodded as Angus spoke, mumbling 'Karen' in between sobs. She placed her tiny hand in his massive one as they made their way to a nearby Red Cross Post where the child's mother was pacing anxiously.

Rosanna stumbled after Angus, glad that Karen's intervention prevented her from revealing a side of her nature that suddenly seemed to be very susceptible to a man who was kind, arrogant, hot then cold, boyish and yet so self-assured. It was very hard to define him in any way.

She watched patiently as he reassured the child's mother, describing himself as a doctor so that she need have no fears about the safety of her daughter while with him. Rosanna smiled, impressed by his manner. She was seeing yet another side of him but felt firmly in control of her body again.

'Let's go over by the lake side of the island ' he offered tersely as the grateful mother thanked him before hugging her little girl. 'I think I've had enough of kids today. A lost child is certainly a mother's worst nightmare.'

'You handled both of them so well, Angus'.

'Thanks, Rosanna.'

He said nothing more, seeming to be quite preoccupied in fact. Sensitive to a change in his mood Rosanna kept quiet feeling that the little incident may have revived memories that he too preferred forget.

∞

The southern side of the small man-made island faced out over the calm blue water of Lake Ontario. There were no waves to mar the smoothness of its surface. By mid-afternoon the sun shone brightly. Like a careless painter's brush stroke, only a few streaky clouds marred the golden blue sky. At the water's edge, yachts bobbled happily at the quayside while families in all shapes, colours, and sizes roamed lackadaisically along the walkway trying to decide which international restaurants would provide the most adventuresome meal.

Rosanna could feel a lessening of tension in the hand that held hers securely. Whatever caused the change in his mood, Angus seemed to be able to overcome it very quickly.

'Would you like to eat in or out, Rosanna?' he asked finally.

'In or out?'

'Indoors or outdoors.' he explained patiently.

'Are they on the menu?' Rosanna questioned pointing at the hundreds of seagulls flying menacingly, waiting for the opportunity to beg or steal some scraps of food.

'We'll eat in I think.' His decision was made after one quick look at Rosanna's distasteful expression but added 'you know I always eat out because it seems to be the thing to do, but I really hate sharing my table with those pesky birds.'

'Italians are famous for eating out of doors and loving it, but,' she paused significantly, 'do you know the old saying *"when in Rome"*?'

Angus frowned, wondering what was coming next, but played along with her offering a tentative and drawn out 'yes'.

'Well, we are not in Rome, so it should be perfectly alright to eat inside.' Laughing she grabbed his arm. 'It's too nice to be serious Angus. We can look at the different menus and decided what country we would like to eat in.'

The last of his introspective mood disappeared as the pair walked casually up and down the quayside before settling on a 50's and 60's style 'hamburger joint' that had an old fashioned soda fountain. Music of the era was played constantly and a small space was set aside for dancing.

'I wish I had been born a bit sooner.' Rosanna sighed wistfully, replete from hamburger, fries, and a strawberry milk shake which she shared with Angus. 'I'm really too young to feel nostalgic about an era that I saw through little girl's eyes. Did you ...?' Rosanna halted. She had been about to ask Angus his age then found that she could not.

'Do you want to know how old I am Rosanna?'

'Yes and no. I mean if you want to tell me, it's ok but I didn't want to pry.' She was clearly flustered.

'I'm not hiding my age. If you think I'm too old for you it would show in more than the number of years on the calendar.' Angus smiled as he spoke. Rosanna was mesmerized by that smile. She followed it up into his eyes;

green eyes that could virtually freeze her respiratory system in overdrive.

'Do you mind Rosanna?'

'Huh?......mind what?' Rosanna wondered if she could be losing her sanity. Every time she looked into his eyes her mental capabilities seemed to desert her.

'That I'm 42'.

'No, of course, I don't mind. Age is not that important to me. As you said, if you were too old it would have shown already. To be honest, Colleen gave the impression that you were much younger than me.' Rosanna felt uncomfortable.

'Sooner or later this guy is going to think that I'm not all there if I keep behaving like a virgin teenager every time he smiles,' Rosanna thought disgustedly. She resolved to get a hold of herself and try to look and act, like a mature woman of thirty-four. Despite her reactions, she agreed to stay on and dance to the old fashioned rock and roll blaring out of a classic juke box.

'This is not going to be like last night, Angus. I was never much good at jiving.'

'Don't need to be. Just follow me and relax.'

Angus was as good as he had been the night before. His hands told her which way to turn with a practiced ease that gave her added confidence.'

After two dances she called a firm halt.

'You make me look good, Angus. I don't know how you do it but I have had enough for today.'

'I really don't want to dance anymore either. We still have a lot of things to see.'

They left the restaurant glowing with the energy of their short dance. They resumed their casual stroll through the park, fingers entwined, while discussing work or work related issues. Occasionally they would stop to admire an exhibit but Angus was talking about his current project. Rosanna was intrigued by the complexity of his research work. She was able to commiserate about the frustrating delays in getting the necessary funding.

'Do you think the grant will be awarded soon Angus?'

'Usually it takes some months. We definitely can't proceed until we get the funding though. I had a very long wait the first time too.'

'If everything is on hold, what would you do in the meantime?'

Angus shrugged in a resigned manner before replying. 'I was a full time pediatrician before I got into genetic research. Right now I'm helping out on peds and the NICU until I hear from the government.'

His reply had given Rosanna food for thought. It explained a lot of his behaviour today with the lost child, his incredible patience and skill with the baby, the previous night. It all seemed at odds with a loner obviously unused to company or companionship. This wasn't the time to discuss his character however. She wanted to know more about his work.

'I know how interesting and challenging pediatrics can be. Why did you switch to genetic research?'

'Too many sick babies! It hurt me deeply to see their suffering especially those born with incurable defects. I got burned out eventually. My chief recognized what was happening and recommended a transfer to the amniocentesis lab. I got to see the early stages of a pregnancy and the development of babies from conception. I just got hooked from there.'

'What kinds of things were you looking for?'

'Primarily lung development. Our hope was to find ways of reducing the need for extensive oxygen therapy, especially for premature births. You know it has consequences for eye development. What I have done, in the past two years, has resulted in some significant changes in protocol. These findings have been confirmed by other studies.'

Rosanna listened intently as he talked on. She loved the work and his obvious commitment to finding answers in a void of knowledge. She understood that research worked only if one could build on an idea. After spending some time working with babies a few years earlier, she understood what would draw him to such a field.

'You are quite remarkable you know.'

'Because I do research?' he queried surprised by her comment.

'No Angus ..... because you care enough to do something about improving the quality of life for a very vulnerable and under-served population.'

Rosanna was jerked back lightly when Angus came to a abrupt halt on the path. When she was facing him he raised the hand captured firmly in his own and kissed it tenderly.

'Thank-you for validating my raison d'être' he uttered softly. 'Sometimes, in the lab we get so caught up in the minor details that we tend to forget the bigger picture and our long term goals.'

Rosanna felt warmed by his appreciation of her comment. They said little, each lost in their own thoughts. The silence was companionable. His long sinewy arm had slipped around her shoulders pulling her closer to the warmth of his body. Her arm soon encircled his trim waist as they moved on, no longer aware of the surroundings, only of each other.

∞

The afternoon merged into early evening with lots of shared talk. Angus was as interested as he was interesting. Neither noticed the increased evening humidity, nor the threat of rain until a few large drops splattered their clothes. It was the kind of summer rainfall that gives a warning then either disappears completely or pours as if the heavens were opened.

'We'd better head for home Rosanna. I don't want you to get wet.

'It may be inevitable anyway. There's such a long walk back to the transit system. Perhaps you are right, though. By the look of the sky, it seems more likely to be a real downpour.'

'It may be alright if we get caught in the bridge on the way back. The rain can't last forever and the bridge is at least covered. Let's go.'

Grabbing her hand again Angus quickened his pace with almost frantic concern. Rosanna was breathless trying to keep pace with his long strides. This was far worse than earlier when he had been only walking. Trying to get him to stop was like pulling teeth.

'Angus please, slow down a little. I can't keep up with you.'

'I'm sorry love, I just don't want you to get wet.'

They reached the end of the long tunnel before the rain fell. It was still some distance to the streetcar terminal but Angus pressed on. It was fruitless. Halfway through the grounds the inevitable happened. Angus was beside himself with dismay.

'Don't fuss please. I won't melt Angus. I have been wet before.'

'I know Rosanna but.....' His tone was testy.

'Does he think I'm made of sugar?' she fumed inwardly, annoyed by his unreasonable and overly protective attitude. Putting her hands on two shapely hips she stopped and looked up into his face through the pouring rain.

'Angus, we are both wet,' she enunciated carefully. 'It's like standing under Niagara Falls. We might as well give in and enjoy it.'

Angus stared at Rosanna as if she lost her senses. In his experience of women, he had never met one like her. He couldn't imagine a woman who would actually endure this, much less enjoy it! He had been prepared for endless complaints, whining, at best a frosty good-night. She was too important to him even after such a short time to risk spoiling a day that had been almost perfect. He wanted to protect and cherish her. As he watched her intently, tell him off in the midst of a summer downpour, he realized the only thing he really wanted to do was to make love to her.

Grabbing her wordlessly, he swooped her up with amazing strength, halting the verbal onslaught with kisses to her eyes, her neck, her nose, and lastly her opened mouth, drinking in the taste of her mingled with the rain.

They were enveloped in a world of cascading water, soaking them through, defining their body curves and angles, heightening their awareness of each other.

'Rosanna, please come home with me?' he pleaded huskily, surprising himself even more than the woman in front of him.

He felt her nodding into his neck as she slid down the length of his body, surely feeling his need of her as he released her slowly. She swayed a bit when he let her go and was soon caught up in his arms again.

'It can be anything you want, Rosanna. I just can't bear to let you go tonight.'

Too bemused to speak, she nodded again, her body naturally gravitating towards him.

'Do you want me to carry you?'

'No! I can walk. I just hadn't realized my feet weren't on the ground until you let me go.' she was finally able to murmur.

Rosanna gave no thought to the words uttered in a literal sense. As they forged ahead through the pouring rain Angus, however, was given food for thought. He hailed a curiously empty taxi near the terminal wondering, silently, if he could ever let her go again.

Chapter 5

The driver of the taxi seemed to be a surly individual.

'Gimme a break,' he exclaimed disdainfully when he stopped in response to Angus' summons. 'You look like a pair of drowned rats. You're gonna mess up my cab.'

'Did you really expect to find someone walking around in dry clothes?'

'Hell no! But I just picked up a couple from home and.....'

'We are not getting any drier standing here.'

The cabby paused, looking them both over with a jaded eye.

'So where you goin'?' he asked. The tone clearly indicated that he did not care about the answer.

Angus gave his address quickly, almost reluctantly and waited for a response that he seemed resigned to hearing for the hundredth time.

'Get right in Boss and your little Missus, too.'

Rosanna raised rain washed eyebrows at the name of the exclusive Queens Quay condominium complex. Questions bubbled at the tip of her tongue. Angus had seen the look. The ardor which had been effectively dampened during the exchange with the driver left him altogether. He sighed knowing some explanation would be necessary.

Rosanna jumped in the cab and folded damp hands in her equally wet lap. She tried to look nonjudgmental. In fact, all she really wanted to do was sneeze. Wherever he lived, she hoped the place was warm. She kept her eyes straight ahead, watching the wipers swish back and forth, his whispered words washing over her, just like the rain.

'Two years ago I won the lottery from a ticket, which I originally bought on a whim. It seemed like good sense to invest in the Harbour View Redevelopment. I've never actually been sorry. In spite of all the hype surrounding the project, my place is just a large bachelor condominium which has a soothing view of the lake.

The word lake sent chills up her spine. The gist of his explanation was unimportant anyway. Rosanna was cold and said little hoping that he wouldn't notice anything beyond the frozen smile on her face.

When she didn't respond beyond an affirmative nod, Angus added no more information. He knew she would see it for herself very soon.

Rosanna shivered both with nervous anticipation and cold.

He said it can be anything I want but what exactly do I want?' she asked her anxious heart.

They soon arrived at the entrance and all decisions were on hold. The opulence of the building was matched by the air cooling system. The wet clothes felt like ice cubes on her skin.

'How high up are you?' she inquired trying to hide her trembling body. The elevator ride seemed endless.

'Your lips are blue!' Angus observed with an air of smugness.

'Ok…ok….. I admit that I'm cold but I asked you how far up do we have to go?' She was testy.

'23 floors….I hope you are not acrophobic Rosanna'

'You are baiting me.' There was a significant pause after her warning tone. 'Ok so you were right and I was wrong but it's not the rain that's bothering me. It's your air conditioning!,' Rosanna admitted out loud *'and my own inability to understand what is happening to me,'* she added silently.

Angus chuckled a bit, but not maliciously. He had baited her. She spurned his protectiveness in the park and his ego had been piqued.

'I didn't want to be right you know. I'd much rather have you safe and warm and comfortable…'

'But Angus……'

'No more buts Rosanna. We're almost there,' he announced as the elevator doors opened. 'I want you in a warm bath as soon as possible.'

Neither missed the embarrassing double entendre. A stiff walk down to his condo was completed in silence. Rosanna gasped with sheer delight at the sight before her as Angus opened the heavy mahogany door.

'What an enormous room!' she exclaimed. 'This space alone could hold my entire one bedroom condo.' Looking around she marveled at the fact that a single room could look like a home and yet contain no walls whatsoever. There were specific designated areas for eating, sleeping and relaxing. The only rooms were the bathroom, closets and storage area near the entrance.

A picture window, running the full length of the room, overlooked the lake, still choppy, with the inclement weather. To her left was the kitchen corner, including a well delineated area for dining but there was no table or chairs. In another corner was a large leather chair flanked by shelves full of reading material and books. A couple of parsons tables were nestled side by side and burdened with piles of papers. The corner desk looked surprisingly neat. In the final corner, a king sized water bed, which looked warm and inviting occupied almost half of one wall. Rosanna was impressed, not so much by the exclusiveness of the unit but by the clever design and layout.

'Look around later. I'm going to set a bath for you,' he said making his way towards the bathroom.

'A shower's fine, Angus.' Rosanna became aware that her body was sending renewed signals of discomfort.

'You'll love this bath. Trust me please. I want to take care of you, at least for tonight.'

He halted at the door, watching earnestly while she stood shivering near the spectacular windows.

'Alright, I do trust you,' she said facing him across the length of the room.

Rosanna was beginning to realize that this man was so different from the males of her family. Without much analysis of the whys or hows, she intuitively found a measure of trust and moved forward to join him. She walked as if in a hypnotic state. Her fingers began to undo the buttons of her blouse. The soggy material next to her skin felt distasteful. Rosanna was in her underwear by the time she reached the impressive white tiled room. Angus was already bent over the elevated jade coloured whirlpool tub fiddling with dials as steam issued invitingly.

'Rosanna hurry up! The bath is ready.'

'I'm right behind you. Don't shout!'

The look on his face was comical as he turned around and saw her nearly nude body, displayed as naturally as if they had been married for years. It was a measure of her confidence in him that she felt no false modesty. She was certain that his 'trust me' meant more than the obvious.

Swallowing hard and determined not to let her down Angus took a deep breath and tried to remember that he was a scientist. Rosanna wasn't a lab specimen. Nothing he had seen in any test tube could excite him the way she did. Just a simple smile was enough. Years of training came to his aid. He suppressed his desires, putting her comfort first.

'Help me with this Angus.'

The wet bra was stuck to her skin. The cold and trembling

fingers were having great difficult with the back fastener. Because he could see that she was tired, he removed it and her panties before guiding her into the hot bubbly spa. She sighed and sank chin deep, fitting her body to the grooves provided, twisting as the jets of warm water began to caress her cold and sluggish body.

'I think I might have died and gone to heaven' she whispered, a tiny part of her religious mind chastising her for the blasphemy.

'I know I am in heaven,' Angus thought contentedly, pleased that he could make her comfortable by providing such a small service.

There was a smaller shower stall in the far corner. He would have loved to share the tub with Rosanna. Angus had given his word though and refused to risk spoiling their fragile relationship by a selfish action. He entered the stall smiling. Despite a frail looking appearance, the athletic and agile man was as healthy as a horse. The thought came and went in his head. It would take more than a little rainstorm to…. the smugness accompanying the thought was soon blown away by a loud sneeze.

Rosanna heard the sneeze and opened her eyes tiredly. She was pleasantly captivated by the tantalizing glimpse of skin visible through the frosted glass. She quickly shut her eyes as the water was turned off. She listened intently for the sound of his movements.

Unable to withstand her curiosity, she opened one eye and observed his unhurried actions with the fluffy white towel. The tight muscles rippled firmly as he bent over. She was fascinated by the perfection of his nude body in motion. Although he was off to her right she nearly got caught peeking at him when he turned suddenly to retrieve his wet clothes from the floor.

Heart pounding, she tried desperately to appear nonchalant. She must have succeeded for he was at her ear whispering softly, so that he wouldn't disturb her, if she had drifted off.

'Rosanna?'

'Hmmmm?'

'Hungry?'

'Gonna cook?' she murmured with a touch of sarcasm.

'Gonna order!' he stated, chuckling. 'Don't be long love. Your face is getting red.' He was gone after a quick peck on the cheek.

Some fifteen minutes later, when she sleepily made her way out of the soothing water, Rosanna found a blue toweling robe behind the door and wrapped it around her glowing body. '*He doesn't do this often*' she reassured herself tying the belt ends firmly around her trim waistline. '*I wonder if he expected me to come out naked.*' 'The possibility of such an action made her giggle nervously. Placing her hands on the washbasin she bit her lip to stop the silly laughter. '*I suppose if he had girls up here regularly, he would have towel, toothbrush, and PJ's handy. Then again,*' she thought, tying the knot a little tighter, '*if I did this often, I would have those things in a large discreet bag!*'

The argument was necessary. Her reflection in the mirror was a worried one. Rosanna was not a virgin. To her everlasting shame, she had surrendered herself to an Australian medical student while they were both studying in England. Virginity was important in her strict Catholic upbringing, a treasure to be saved for marriage. Loneliness, the reality of being away from hom and modern life, had dimmed the gilt on the treasure. Derek, a psychologically abusive lover, had quickly rearranged her values to suit himself. He finished his studies and returned to Australia without a word of remorse, leaving her frightened, heartbroken, and caught in an emotional vacuum. Low marks, for the first time in her academic life snapped her out of a near suicidal depression, but she bore the scar for years.

In her maturity, she had a better perspective on relationships. Time had also lessened the hurt but not the memory. Dates were strictly platonic. *'Perhaps that's why I am attracted to Angus. He's shown me that he wants me but he hasn't been aggressively sexual. We haven't known each other long,'* she mused, smiling at the dark haired girl reflected in the mirror. *'Barely 24 hours but he's so kind. I feel like I have known him for years.'* The fresh scrubbed oval face grinned foolishly back at her.

Her reflections had wasted a fair amount of time. She was startled back to reality by a gentle rap on the door.

'I'm done Angus. I'll be right there.'

'How courteous he is. After we have already shared this room he still has the decency to knock.' Rosanna fluffed up her hair, trying to affect some semblance of a style before giving up completely. Instead, she rinsed with mouth wash from a bottle on the counter and left the haven of the bathroom, only a little bit reluctantly.

She couldn't see Angus at first but noted that he had turned off the air-conditioner. Rosanna made her way, tentatively, into the main part of the room looking around for the blond head.

'Angus?'

'I'm here...in the easy chair.'

She padded barefoot in the direction of the voice. In the background she heard the sound of a clothes dryer.

'Is there no end to his consideration?'

Rosanna found him looking comfortable and relaxed in a pair of pale blue boxer shorts, a white unadorned T-shirt, sitting, legs up on the matching footstool. There was an opened book in his lap. The reading glasses were perched on top. He motioned for her to join him. Rosanna made her way to sit down on the large foot rest. Angus held out his arms and offered a silent invitation for her to join him in the chair. Her hesitation was only a fraction of a second before she occupied his quickly vacated lap. She curled up against his chest, resting her head under his chin. Long arms which had held her on the dance floor now enveloped her firmly.

'Are you hungry now?'

'Ravenous!'

'I'll have to learn to cook, I think.'

Rosanna pulled back her head searching his face to see if he were serious. He was, or at least appeared to be. Their eyes locked and held. The soft light from the reading lamp created an intimate glow. The spectacular view from the window was forgotten.

One soft, trembling hand touched an angular jaw

encouraging it to move closer. As before, the kiss was a mere meeting of lips. His sudden passion in the park seemed to have failed him. Instead, his free hand moved to explore the thick lashes which had so entranced him. He stroked the lips that could create such havoc in his groin. The feathery caress invited a return of the smile. On cue, the lips parted as willed, not provocatively but lovingly. Rosanna was feeling well disposed towards him. His kindness had touched her deeply.

Their lips met again lightly, still learning. The kiss ended but not the lingering gaze. Breathing patterns changed, stirring feelings that neither understood clearly. Angus knew that he felt as close to loving this woman as possible. Rosanna wasn't sure and a gentle frown marred the smooth brow.

Angus saw the worry lines. His finger tip replaced the pressure of his lips. It did not stop long but moved slowly about the oval face as he watched the play of emotions in her features.

The bow lips parted again as he traced the lower line then relaxed as the finger climbed the rise of her cheek. There was a barely perceptible pause then a slow meander, sliding down the column of her neck. He stopped to realign his perceptions of the beauty before him.

She captured the hand as it stilled and stared at the fingers. Rosanna loved the length of them, remembering the way they held the small baby, firmly but gently. She stroked each one and gave into the desire to plant a soft kiss in the palm, before placing it at the side of her face. A light squeeze said volumes about feelings, as yet unexpressed.

Angus received the silent message and his look became less clinical and more loving as the journey continued through the hollow at the neck, rising to the peak of the sun kissed shoulders before the hand gently rested in the valley between her breasts. The light brown tip invited his touch but he hesitated, waiting to be invited to explore its softness.

Rosanna stirred in his lap, aware of his increasing need. She knew her movements were unlikely to ease anyone's discomfort.

'You look so good in blue,' he murmured huskily sliding the terry towel cloth from her shoulders. He encountered no resistance and his indrawn breath, filled with awe, set her heart racing.

They kissed again, mouths opened, tongues seeking. Now the pressure was unbearable. The surge of desire between them ignited suddenly into unendurable want. She rocked her body in his lap, seeking something more, each lost to all thought but the need to be in each other's arms. An insistent buzzing sound finally permeated the cotton wool of desire surrounding the couple in the chair.

'Angus....Angus...the door' she gasped.

'Oh damn, not now...... not now.'

Realizing the futility of trying to ignore the summons, Angus released the taut breast that he had been holding. Reluctantly he detached himself from her lips. He slid his free hand under her thighs and stood up carrying her to the door on sure feet. He didn't want to let her go.

'You don't need to carry me. Please put me down '

I don't want to my love. I never want to. I'll just tell the guy to go to he...', he announced releasing her reluctantly.

'You called him didn't you?' she interrupted, encouraging him to press the intercom and let in the delivery man.

'I did, but I don't want his food anymore. I want you instead.'

Rosanna sighed, letting out a long pent up breath. Her blood had been fired to strange new heights but underneath the desire lay a very real hunger and a caution telling her to slow the pace. She wanted Angus physically. There was no doubt in her mind or body. She was surprised to find herself overwhelmed by the depth of desire in both of them, yet understood the need to put on the brakes, if only temporarily.

'I have to eat Angus. We Italians have a deep attachment to food. Making love on an empty stomach is just not done.'

Angus laughed, as she hoped he would. 'I'm sorry. I guess I acted more or less like....'

'We both acted.'

'We both got a little carried away then.'

They exchanged a short kiss before he released her to pay the indignant delivery man who mumbled incomprehensively before stomping off. Clearly he was not at all mollified by the generous tip and profuse apologies.

Desire continued to wane in the face of the delicious aroma emanating from the bags placed on the counter in the kitchen. There was no comfortable place to sit. A blanket was spread on the floor to serve as table and chairs. They took time to sort out the boxes of food, disdaining the formality of plates.

'Really Angus, how do you manage?' Rosanna mumbled, her eyes crossing charmingly as a large shrimp, anchored between chopsticks, suddenly appeared in front of her. Like everything else he did, Angus maneuvered them quite deftly.

'Never had to bother much.'

For the first time, Rosanna got a real glimpse of the loneliness behind the shrug. She opened her mouth to make another comment on the lack of basic amenities when she found it full of very fine noodles. She gave up trying to talk altogether and accepted each mouthful like a dutiful child, happier and more content than she had been in a long time.

Chapter 6

The exchange of food, in the unorthodox impromptu meal, started as soon as Rosanna was able to discard the last of her inhibitions. Sticky fingers found his mouth open and waiting for the sweet and sour pork bits hidden among the ginger flavored vegetables. Their burgeoning sexuality had not been fully contained. It was simply transferred to another realm. Rosanna was finding it far more sensual to be feeding each other.

There was enough food to satisfy a small family but they were able to do justice to the feast. It was clear that Angus had a good appetite. At each meal they shared in their short relationship he always ate well. Rosanna had a great metabolism but she knew that a few more meals like the one she was sharing would result in any number of unwanted pounds.

'Please Angus, no more I feel like I'm going to burst,' Rosanna gasped at the end of what seemed to be a marathon of eating.

'Are you sure? This stuff won't taste good tomorrow,' he grinned at her, searching around for more tempting bits and pieces in a sea of gravy and salty sauces.

The word tomorrow gave her a pang. She ignored it.

'Yes I'm sure. What I need now is something to drink.'

Angus dug into one of the bags and held up two tins in the familiar colours of a popular soft drink company.

'Not diet soda! After such a wonderful meal, are we are going to drink diet soda!?'

Angus wanted to laugh but felt it would be inappropriate. He realized that not only food but its presentation was important to her. No matter how careless he was with his own dietary habits, she viewed things differently. He tried to coax a compromise from her.

'We can always pretend its champagne.' She didn't look impressed with the idea. He bowed his head before looking up at her again. 'Sometimes we have to pretend a lot to get through life. There is always a small world of imagination and make-believe hidden away in all of us. We suppress it but we can't lose it. Close your eyes Rosanna. You'll be able to create anything you want, in your mind's eye and transfer it to real life, if you believe in possibilities and miracles.'

Angus's voice was compelling, as if the words were drawn from a distant well at the core of his soul. Without question, she understood the deeper meaning and could not ignore the hypnotic, seductive inflection. Rosanna sipped the cold bubbly liquid through a straw closing her eyes as the carbonated drink tickled her nose. When she opened them again, his gaze was locked on her face. The gentle coaxing expression had been replaced by one of desire. She said nothing, only returning his look, her head tilted to the side, the dark hair falling over one shoulder.

'Are you full now Rosanna?'

'Yes...yes I am.'

'Stay here' he commanded kindly.

She watched as he moved to clear up the mess left from the boxes. He refused her silent offer of help. When he was done, Angus offered her a hand-up off the floor. She excused herself to go to the bathroom where she nervously washed her hands and mouth. With a deep tremulous sigh, Rosanna opened the door and returned to the edge of the large bed. Angus waited patiently at its other side. She stopped and faced him across the width of it.

Neither made a move to initiate the act which had seemed to be a foregone conclusion such a short time ago. They were both floundering in a situation where each obviously lacked the experience to proceed. They wanted to be in each other's arms but hesitated until the delay was almost becoming an embarrassment. A series of expressions crossed Rosanna's face giving a clear indication that she had no wish to make a fool of herself.

Angus shifted from foot to foot wondering suddenly where his common sense had gone. *'How could I hope to seduce a woman like Rosanna?'*

He had never enjoyed a serious relationship in his life. He knew that he wanted her more than he ever wanted any woman, but was so afraid of failure. Angus, the man, felt himself wallowing in the midst of a self-fulfilling prophecy.

As he watched her standing at the other side of his bed the scientist knew only one thing clearly. He already cared deeply about her and he had to find a way to tell her. This time, he chose words over action, an approach which was endearing to the nervous woman.

'Please, come here Rosanna.' he pleaded softly, extending his hand across to her, 'I want to show you something.'

Rosanna made her way around the bed, tightening the bathrobe as she padded towards his outstretched hand. He drew her gently in front of him, facing out to the wide expanse of the window to enjoy the view under the dark but clearing skies. No words passed between them as they watched unidentified, winking lights in the horizon, send unknown messages to an invisible and fathomless receptacle. Time passed, unheeded as they began to point out places of interest and highly visible landmarks. Nothing held their interest as much as the moon, which shone brightly against the backdrop of the black sky.

'It's so incredibly beautiful Angus,' Rosanna sighed, feeling secure, wrapped warmly in his non threatening embrace.

'It is lovely, although I'm not really looking at the scene before me. Its beauty pales behind the reflection of you in the glass.'

Rosanna felt an unknown tremor course through her body. She knew that she wanted this wonderful man to make love to her. He seemed as hesitant as she was. While looking at him across the bed, she realized that he harbored as many uncertainties as she did.

'What experiences did he have,' she wondered, *'which could make him afraid of revealing himself?'*

Rosanna had no false confidence when it came to sex. She had been badly hurt, was on the shelf in the marriage market as far as her parents were concerned and yet she knew instinctively that Angus would not reject or abuse her if she failed to measure up. *'Is it me or himself that he doesn't trust?'* she wondered idly.

The strong arms clutched firmly around her waist tensed, reminding Rosanna that Angus had paid her a compliment. She had not responded except to sigh. Her head moved back to rest against his shoulder. As her body relaxed with the reassuring gesture, she felt a similar physical response in him.

'You make me feel really special because you have a way with words Angus.' She covered his hands with her own as she spoke adding extra warmth to her delayed reply.

'I disagree with you. Whatever words I've found, you put them there. I've never been known as a particularly talkative type of guy. In fact....' he halted, knowing that she would feel his tortuous indrawn breath. Angus was unable to stop its pull. When he covered up the threat of tears, already stinging behind his eyes, he continued softly, finding the courage to speak from his heart without self pity. 'More than a few of my acquaintances would be surprised to know that I even have a woman here at all.'

Rosanna frowned realizing what the admission must have cost him. Remembering her own first impressions, it was not a startling confession. She dug deep inside of herself to find the right response so that the fragile threads of their growing relationship could hold firmly.

'You are a very private person Angus. I can sense that about you, even in such a short time. You seem to be introspective and perhaps lonely, as I am. Maybe it stems from the type of work that we do.' She paused before completing her statement. 'It has been almost eight years since I've been this intimate with a man, but you've touched me physically and emotionally in ways I didn't think possible.'

She made to turn around, wanting to reassure him with a look but he forestalled her by gently loosening the knot in the robe.

'I am shocked to find that I care so deeply for you after such a short time. Nothing like this has ever happened to me before but neither... "my five wits nor my five senses can dissuade one foolish heart from serving thee."

'Shakespeare too Angus? How lovely!' Rosanna felt her heart melting. She had always used phrases from the sonnets to make biting comments. This felt so different. He knew she loved the words of the great Bard. Closing her eyes, she swayed gently listening to the seductive tenor of his voice as he continued.

'I don't want to just make love to you Rosanna, I want to love you too. Maybe it's too soon for you to reciprocate; it doesn't even matter right now. Somehow, I'm not worried about the future, only the present. Your words have .....your understanding h........'

She murmured for him to hush. She truly understood not only his feelings but the importance of the moment. She couldn't be sure of her feelings. It was too soon, but she was satisfied that she did care deeply about him, desired him above all else at that moment and needed to solidify that feeling physically. She finished untying the knot and eased away from him to allow the robe to slide easily to the floor.

She observed his movements reflected in the window. Circular caresses over the smooth skin were unhurried. He seemed to enjoy the silky feel of it. The palm of his hand made several lights forays over the line of the rib cage and down to the shapely waist where his large hands could almost span its width. The hips were large, but firm and well rounded.

Rosanna could feel her own intake of breath when the hands travelled upwards encircling the firm globes of her breast. Her head fell back against his chest allowing him access to the creamy contours of her neck. He ran his tongue lightly over the smooth skin. She reveled in the feel of the rough surface of his tongue.

It didn't take long for her body to resonate sensuously to his ministrations, the shoulders rising and falling, her head twisting and turning. Her breath seemed to stop completely as the hand moved down once more encountering the brunette hair, tantalizingly soft, which covered her womanly secrets.

He found his way easily past the dark curtain, ineffective against his probing fingers. There was no tension or stress. They rocked in each other's arms, swaying to the music unheard, but felt by lovers for years. As his hands and fingers gently exorcised the ghosts of her past, she sighed tremulously, enjoying the light rhythmic feel of him against the swollen and aching tissue. Unable to withstand the assault without some measure of reciprocation, she turned sharply finding his mouth unerringly, and allowing his arousal to replace his fingers as she stood on her toes before him.

Rosanna gasped at the feel of Angus. Digging her fingers in his shoulders she wondered how anyone could doubt the very maleness of him. His length was doing wondrous things to her body. She wound her arms around his neck holding tightly as sensation after sensation rocked her body. She strained upward wanting the feel of him inside her. With minimum effort her legs soon found themselves wrapped around his torso. His deceptive strength had lifted her allowing his firmness to enter the moist pulsating core of her womanhood.

She moaned as the unfamiliar fullness seemed to reach to the depth of her body, pulsating wildly with a life of its own. Rosanna felt that she could have stayed as she was forever but Angus couldn't support her weight. He turned allowing her to rest her legs on the bed. He kissed the tips of the puckered nipples before encouraging her to lie down.

He seemed in no hurry to join her but stood watching her lovingly as she lay on her side not provocatively but expressing a frank sexual need mixed with an old-fashioned modesty. The pause was enough to allow her to think of the consequences of what they were going to do. In her ignorance, she'd had a close call before which was later attributed to the depression but......

'Angus, I'm not on the pill.' she whispered softly not wanting to spoil the moment, but knowing that it could present some difficulties.

'I'll take care of it Rosanna.' he mumbled leaning over to extract a small foil package from the bedside table. He had to search a bit and seemed almost embarrassed to find one. He settled himself, lying on his side, facing her.

'I want to see you when I make love to you Rosanna. Your face is so expressive. It makes me feel so good to see your emotion. Does it bother you if I tell you?'

'No, somehow it makes me feel really wanted, really needed.'

She moved across the small space between them to plant a light kiss on his lips. He welcomed her, deepening the kiss as his hand strayed up and down the rise and fall from hip to thigh. When he encountered her knee, he lifted her leg over his own, giving him access to her moist essence.

'Don't make me wait any longer Angus' she gasped as his fingers continued to access the core of her sexuality. He obliged, guiding himself into her with a teasing slowness that was almost his undoing. His body jerked spasmodically while he held her shoulders breathing deeply, trying to control himself and prevent an immediate release.

'Is anything wrong?' Rosanna asked softly. 'Are you in pain?'

'Only the pain of not having you in my life before now. I have waited so long for this, for you, I just don't want it to be over before we can enjoy it.'

Rosanna subsided. She was inexperienced, hadn't realized the subtleties of making love, but thanked God that Angus was different enough to be patient with her naivety. She felt his trembling hand smooth the hair away from her face while he kissed her lightly on her eyes, her nose and her parted lips.

When he was ready, he placed his hand at the small of her back guiding her to him while he responded with long, slow, agonizingly beautiful movements of his hips. He watched her face intently, enjoying the contortions of her face as the rhythmic movements seemed to flow upward flooding her with heat, suffusing her entire being with desire. They were totally in tune sexually. Just as they had been on the dance floor, Angus timed each thrust with a perfect cadence. Each stroke filled her with languorous ease, meeting the response of her increasing rise to the peak of fulfillment. Rosanna's hand cupped his face, bringing it near enough for a kiss without changing the soft pattern of their lovemaking. Her body arched sharply as she felt the unbearable and unfamiliar tingling sensation of an approaching climax.

Her lips begged for his ministration and he bent his head to caress their soft moistness so close to him, even as the pressure for his own release pounded in his low back. Rosanna moaned pitifully, squeezing his shoulders as she alternatively pushed him away then pulled him to her, kneading at the bulging muscles in his shoulders, taut with tension. She was unsure of the response overtaking her body but felt safe in his arms.

'Love me Angus......more...please,' she pleaded as her roller coast ride to satisfaction scaled the final rise then toppled headlong leaving its passengers floating then gliding. She never knew when Angus joined her. She only felt a warmth and tenderness deep inside as she clung to his body.

Neither participant seemed to have any awareness of the end of the ride. Both were stunned by the natural release of sexual tension which had held them spellbound. Their eyes were locked as tightly as the hands holding each other's body. Their mingling breaths were deep and tortured. They had no desire to separate their bodies from each other. Rosanna couldn't speak. She continued to hold him firmly, crying softly between punctuated kisses for the beauty of the experience they shared.

'I never knew this intimacy could be so wonderful Angus.

I have never felt like this before,' she eventually whispered into his ear.

'Would you believe me if I told you I feel exactly the same. How is it that we could discover this wonderful feeling in each other? I am lost for words.'

His hands continued to stroke her hair, face and body, held tightly in his arms. Angus had no awareness of one second beyond the moment he was feeling. An urge to recreate the sensations rose in him again. He couldn't hide the fact of his desire any more than he could have resisted her before.

Rosanna felt his burgeoning need return and held him tightly in her body giving little care to the unusual circumstances and the brevity of their relationship. She only knew that her body was fired by his responding passion and, he alone, could satisfy her need. She rolled on to her back and waited for a heart stopping instant as he towered above her. The provocative smile she offered in her lips and the innocence of her eyes held him captive.

Angus was as gentle as he had been before, but startling her with the beauty of his male power in the dominant position. All the gentle feminine things he had done for her comfort faded, to be replaced by a primitive surge in her womanhood to meet his wholly masculine driving energy. The peak was filled with power, as the two collided in that vortex of time and space where only desire, fired by love, exists.

Sighs and whimpers faded ever so slowly, as the black night enveloped them in a cocoon of sleep, wrapped in each other's arms.

Chapter 7

'Where am I?' Rosanna thought, feeling totally disoriented. *'I must have fallen asleep in the bath. Why do I feel like I'm on a boat?'*

Because she so often woke up at odd hours, her usual practice was to prepare herself mentally before bed. She couldn't focus in on the day or the time and felt a familiar feeling of panic begin to well up inside her. It seemed like an impossible task to open her eyes. As she became aware of a long arm tightly wrapped around her naked body she screamed, flying out of bed as if she were being attacked by the big ugly roaches that often invaded her nightmares when she was overtired.

Angus, startled out of sleep by the sudden action, opened one eye cautiously. The face of Rosanna stood out starkly, a vision of fear with eyes like saucers. She was hyperventilating alarmingly. He understood her disorientation. Night work fatigue, and over stimulation often produced totally irrational responses.

'Easy…easy, Rosanna. It's me Angus.'

He didn't touch her but jumped up out of bed ready to catch her in case she fell. He continued to croon soothingly. 'You're at my apartment Rosanna. It's Sunday morning.' He was about to grab for the proverbial brown bag, when the dangerously rapid breathing began to slow. Her colour was improving too.

'Oh Angus,' she gasped finally. 'I'm really sorry. This happens to me sometimes. Usually I'm fine once I can get my eyes open and see a clock in a familiar place. I just couldn't focus on anything except the feel of your arm. It panicked me a bit.'

'Don't apologize dearest.' He continued to whisper soothingly, gathering her into his arms. 'It has happened to me before. Too much night work does have that effect.'

It wasn't time for sexuality. He retrieved the blue terry robe from the floor and placed it around her shoulders. A light peck on her forehead added a small touch of unthreatening comfort.

'Go to the bathroom and wash up. You'll find an unused toothbrush in the cabinet. There's some extra towels and stuff in the cupboard beside the shower. Help yourself to anything you need.' His words were delivered in an even matter of fact tone. Any lingering fear dissipated quickly. She shot him a grateful glance, which he misinterpreted.

'No I won't join you now. I plan to fix breakfast.' Her initial look of thanks changed to a pout with his first statement, then one of surprise with his second.

'Are you sure you are alright now?' Clearly, Angus was ignoring the obvious.

'Yes I'm sure and you know very well why I look like this.'

'Never mind,' he grinned, pushing her towards the door. 'And take your time!'

Thirty minutes later, Rosanna emerged from the bathroom feeling at peace with herself and the world. She had taken a hot and soothing shower, washed her hair and refused to dwell on any aspect of the unusual circumstances except the happiness that Angus brought into her dreary life in such a short time. The whole weekend could turn out to be dream but at least it would be the best one that she had in a very long time. A lack of self-consciousness about the depth of their intimacy surprised her. Deep inside, Rosanna felt as if Angus had always been a part of her life.

The smell of fresh coffee assailed her nostrils as soon as she opened the door.

'Did you lie to me Angus?' Hands on hips she was ready to confront him for his apparent food perfidy.

'I'd never lie to you. I ordered from the restaurant take out service downstairs. I did fix it up on the floor.'

As Rosanna approached their makeshift table, she could see threads of crisp fried bacon, golden brown pancakes swimming in maple syrup, fresh orange juice and blueberry muffins still steaming beside a pat of butter. She smiled at his expression.

'It really does look good.'

'Well, sit down before it gets cold.'

The large terry robe had been comfortable the previous night when the pair cocooned themselves in the muted light of the condo but in the early morning, with the sun shining mercilessly through the picture window, Rosanna felt suddenly shy about getting down to the floor without appearing provocative.

Sensing her discomfiture, Angus got up. 'I'll just wash up and then come back. Go ahead and start. I won't be a minute.'

'I just can't believe how sensitive he is. Where has he been all my life?' Rosanna felt near to tears. She held them inside, waited until he rejoined her then tucked into the breakfast giving full justice to it.

It was a relaxed meal. Very little conversation passed between them. Despite the differences in stature and temperament, Rosanna and Angus had healthy appetites and ate with a real appreciation of the food, sharing and feeding each other as they had done the previous night. They reminisced about childhood meals, punctuating their stories with unrestrained laughter. Rosanna began to wonder where the woman inside her had been hiding for so long. Together they cleared up the dishes then returned to the large comfy chair by mutual consent. The newly acquainted couple still had a lot to learn about each other. Surprisingly neither felt the pull of sexuality, although it lingered just below the surface of their movements.

As Rosanna sat cozily in his lap, her head resting against his shoulder, his arms tightened around her body. She only wished at that moment to hold time in abeyance, to keep the world from intruding and to give this fragile relationship a chance to nurture itself. With the sun shining firmly on them through the window she felt as if time were indeed standing still. Nothing of the real world was visible to mar the perfection of the moment. Only the blue sky, clear and undemanding, intruded unobtrusively.

'Angus, tell me about your family? Not Colleen, but your parents and siblings.'

He didn't balk at the question, but spoke absentmindedly as if his thoughts were elsewhere. The hand stroking her back was soothing with its rhythmic circular movement. 'There are four of us…two girls and two boys. I'm the oldest but after I was born in Scotland, my parents waited until they immigrated to Canada before my sisters Megan and Morag were born.'

'Are they twins?'

'Yes,' he said nodding tenderly at their memory. 'They were premature, Megan being the oldest by twelve minutes.'

'Any problems?

'Oh yes.' He nodded and paused. Clearly the story revived deep memories. 'I was seven at the time. They seemed so tiny to me. Both of them spent weeks in the hospital after they were born. The girls had some eye damage from the oxygen and Morag is in fact legally blind. She can see shapes and shadows in a narrow frame. Meagan, who weighed a little more at birth was a bit healthier, and needed less oxygen. She sees well enough with her glasses. Meg is married to a wonderful guy. He's also a doctor. A nicer man, I have yet to meet. They love each other deeply but a specialist ruled out children for her and Sam.'

'May I ask why?'

'Mostly physical issues. Meagan is aware that her muscular weakness does not prevent her from having a child, but the pregnancy itself would be too debilitating. They may adopt an older child at some point.'

'Are they happy Angus?'

'Very much. When I had my big win, I helped to set up Sam in his GP's office and Meagan does his reception work. There was no bragging in his tone, just a sense of pride for his sister's happiness and achievements.

'What about Morag?'

'She's a minx. She works at the CNIB office and dates a fellow there. She's also my best date. Her boyfriend Mark doesn't dance and she loves it, so I take her out as often as possible.'

'You are a superb dancer. Did you learn because your sister loved it?'

'In the beginning, she didn't love it at all. Morag also has mild Cerebral Palsy. Her physiotherapist drew me aside and told me that dancing would help her to get a better sense of balance as her sight faded. I lied to her, and gave the impression that she was helping me.'

'You've really been their protector haven't you?' Rosanna commented thinking of her own older brother Dominic and his overly protective attitude towards her.

'They needed no crusading defender' he averred modestly. 'Both of them are gutsy girls and made their way despite the handicaps.'

'And your brother?'

Angus shifted in the chair, frowning at some remembered pain. He took a deep tremulous breath before continuing.

'Ian was born four years after the girls. I'm afraid that in the early days I didn't have much time for him and he badgered me unmercifully.'

Rosanna, who had younger brothers and sisters, two of them fraternal twins, understood the difficulties of sibling rivalry. She did however sense a deeper problem, beyond the normal bickering of childhood.

'Why was he like that?'

'I spent so much time caring for the girls that I never had much time for myself or Ian. Dad was really the one who tended to him. Mum had to work and when she was home the girls occupied most of her time. She trusted me to be her helper because I had no fear of their disabilities. She left them in my care quite often but our activities couldn't include Ian who didn't understand his own strength.

'It wasn't wasted time Angus. You seem to care so much about your work, the budding pediatrician probably developed from those days.'

'Yes, I think so' he agreed, delighted by her perception.

'Have you mended fences with Ian?'

'No...' Angus paused for a long time. She didn't say more, waiting and giving him a chance to discuss why the relationship had not been resolved. She hoped he would trust her enough to talk freely.

Angus turned away to look out the window. 'When I won the money, Ian was a junior minister at the church and newly married. He and Sarah were planning to go to South America as missionaries, for three years to help in some of the poorer communities. He felt I should make a contribution and I did, initially. He was put out by the size of the donation, feeling that it wasn't commensurate with the total amount I had received.'

'But shouldn't they be grateful for any amount, in the true spirit of giving?'

'I thought so too. I was wrong. When I realized the depth of his anger, I enlisted the help of several friends and raised nearly an equal amount in cash and clothes, but he still wasn't satisfied.'

'I'm sorry Angus….'

'I am too. He exploded one night and told me in no uncertain terms that the Church was doing its best to help people like me and I should have contributed twice as much, half being my own personal endowment.'

Rosanna gasped at the insult, incredulous that a brother and a man of the cloth could be so self righteous. She felt her temper rising for the hurt inflicted on the man who held her so firmly, but quashed any verbal onslaught. She realized that it had nothing to do with religion, and certainly nothing to do with her. It was merely the action of a jealous and hurt younger brother lashing out for past injustices, real and imagined.

Clearly the hurt had gone deeply on both sides. There was a suspicious moistness in the eyes of the man who was becoming dearer to her each minute that she spent in his company.

'Does Ian realize that the assertions he made are not true Angus?'

'I have never denied or affirmed his beliefs about me. It's up to Ian to come to terms with his unjust opinions. I know what and who I am.' There was finality in his tone indicating that the subject was closed.

'Thank you for sharing that with me.' she whispered.

Angus held her tightly, saying nothing for a long time. She was content to lie there, offering what comfort she could by her silent presence. It took some time for Angus to return to an awareness of her. His hand, moving with a life of its own, ceased it circular movement and began to stroke the thick hair, allowing its heaviness to fall through his fingers. Rosanna felt a lessening of tension as the minutes ticked away unheeded. Relaxed and comfortable in his arms, she soon realized that the stroking had an insistent rhythmic pattern. Memory of their lovemaking the previous night returned full force, almost stopping her breath with its intensity. Rosanna was getting restless, eager to abandon all common sense, when the hand stilled suddenly leaving her baffled and disappointed.

He had been such a wonderful lover. She wondered if he was having doubts about his masculinity after revealing such intimate pain. Rosanna was at loss. She was too inexperienced to understand the psyche of the masculine ego with respect to sex. All the men in her life were aggressive, demanding, macho males. They would balk at someone, like Angus, who wasn't afraid to display sensitivity. She felt a tiny prickle of fear.

'Let's go to the whirlpool. I need to relax.'

It wasn't what she expected him to say. If the ghosts of his past were haunting him she knew intuitively that sex would probably be a better exorcist, but she still had a lot to learn about him and herself. He smiled tiredly at her concerned face, but offered no further comment as they made their way to the bathroom. Rosanna swallowed her hurt and disappointment following his lead.

They sat for some time in the heated water. The previous night Rosanna had avoided the pulsating jets of water hitting her low back and breasts. She had been afraid of the sensual stimulation. Today for some reason, she reveled in it, hoping that Angus would feel the same. He seemed very absorbed by the sight of her bobbing breasts on the surface of the water. Still he made no move to touch her.

'Angus?'

His name was almost a blatant plea from her lips. Few men could have resisted what was being offered. Angus seemed to remain unmoved. Rosanna had just about enough when he spoke up.

'Rosanna, my dearest, do you believe that I don't want to make love to you?' He didn't wait for the obvious answer. 'I do, desperately! But, I don't have any more protection and I….'

'Protection? You mean you don't have any more condoms?' She felt heat begin to rise in her.

'Yessss….'

'Oh you fool!' she laughed closing the gap between them with indecent haste. 'Why didn't you just tell me that? I trust you to do the right thing with nature's contraceptive.'

'I'm not sure if I trust myself. I am beyond waiting now.' He reached out his arms pulling her closer and guiding her onto his length in one swift move.

'How could you hope to hide this from me?' she challenged into his ear.

'I never wanted to…..' Angus couldn't complete the sentence for she rode him light as a feather in the heated pool of water. It didn't take long for their body temperature to rise alarmingly above that of the surrounding water.

Droplets splashed everywhere, creating a wild and exciting coupling that aroused them both to a fever pitch. Their heads were thrown back, faces taut with emotion.

When it was time, his fingers gripped her buttocks tightly praying that he would have the strength to withdraw at the right time.

'Tell me…tell me when…I ..' Rosanna lost the ability to speak as the biggest wave overpowered her senses. Angus grunted in response then gasped, almost wheezing with the force of his excitement. He gave her body a none to gentle push upwards when it was time. Her own hand quickly found his throbbing length. She held him firmly in an effort to compensate for the loss of her inner warmth. She kissed him deeply as the final pulse pounded in his back.

'Did you miss me?' she questioned teasingly when their breathing pattern returned to normal.

'A little, but thanks for what you did. It made things…. a lot easier for me.'

They hugged and hugged, rocking back and forth. Rosanna

buried her face in his neck effectively hiding the tears of joy which could not be held back.

For his part, Angus was shocked by the man inside of him, who had risen from sexual death by the proximity of the woman in his arms. He couldn't imagine that his 'unawakened' lover's soul could be so nurtured by her kindness. What he was feeling brought him to an almost complete thaw of his former frozen self. To be breathless in her arms was better than the unfeeling automon he had become.

In the aftermath of their coupling, the lovers felt real time fade into a nothingness bubble effectively dividing them from the outside.

∞

'Is that the phone Angus?' she asked sometime later, feeling delirious as their locked bodies floated aimlessly through the water.

'I'm afraid so. I have to answer it sweetheart. It could be the hospital.' He quickly jumped out of the tub, leaving a trail of wet footprints on the floor.

'Are you on call?'

'Only if the senior resident runs into a problem which he is unable to handle or if the first team is out on a case. If it's the hospital, I may be tied up for hours.' he threw over his shoulder while picking up the handset.

Rosanna dried herself off and joined Angus by the phone a spare towel in her hand. She wiped off his body, even as he listened. At one point he smiled, thankful for her ministrations before speaking to the caller.

'What is the estimated time of arrival? Do we know the status of the mother? Yes!….yes….get Roger Winstone on the phone and see if he would be prepared to come in. We may have to operate if the babies are stable.'

There was a pause while Angus listened before speaking again. 'Any chance that a family member will be there?'

Another long pause followed before he said briskly, 'Good, I'm on my way.'

Rosanna knew the real world had intruded on her fantasy weekend.

'I don't have to tell you what's happened,' he said, accepting the towel to finish drying his body quickly.

'No…is it something unusual?'

'Yes, boys conjoined at the hip and chest, undiagnosed because of the lack of facilities available in their community. They are being flown in from Nunavut. There doesn't seem to be any genetic abnormality, just a separation accident but they are also quite premature. They were fortunate a surgeon happened to be nearby when she went into labor.'

'I hope their connection is just on the surface. Life will be easier if they don't share major organs. It must be terrifying for the parents to deal with this, then face losing them to distance as well.'

'I knew you were the right girl for me Rosanna.' He held her shoulders and kissed her. He was already becoming distracted, his mind on the tasks ahead. 'I'll call you, as soon as I know how long I'll be.'

'I won't stay here and wait Angus, I must go home.'

'I hate for you to leave but if you must, let me drop you off.'

'I would appreciate that.' Rosanna was already donning her shorts. They had been forgotten in the drier and felt cold and unfamiliar. 'I have neglected my family this weekend and they won't be pleased.'

'Will they mind much?'

'They will mind a lot!'

Angus hesitated while buttoning his shirt. He left it undone and walked over to her. A warm hug brought her close to his body. He felt her softness. The memory of their lovemaking was already imprinted on every inch of him. Taking her shoulders, he sought those beautiful eyes.

'I hope to meet them someday soon Rosanna.'

'I hope so too, but it won't be as straight forward as you think. They are still very Italian.'

Rosanna said no more. She refused to meet his eyes, instead occupying her attention with the top button of his shirt and the hairy cluster visible beneath.

'I'm not worried.'

'The supreme confidence of the ignorant,' she laughed moving away from the pull of his body, feeling happy to know that he wasn't offended.

'I'm ready Angus' she said a few minutes later. 'Let's go!'

There was one last kiss at the door. 'They'll wonder what's come over me.'

'Why?'

'I haven't driven to work in seven years!'

Chapter 8

Rosanna hobbled from foot to foot as she waited impatiently for the elevator in her building. She longed for the privacy and familiarity of her apartment so that she could review and analyze the events of the weekend. She wrapped her arms tightly around her torso as a wave of sensual delight washed over her at the memories. Glancing around she hoped no one would notice.

'They will probably think I need a ladies room anyway,' she thought. *'Everything I've done seems so strange and unreal. Was I really that abandoned woman in the hot tub?'*

Her face burned at the memory. Glancing around again, her eye caught the mailbox. Both elevators seemed to be stuck on the upper floors so Rosanna hurried over to see if she had any letters. The box was full! Work had been distracting. She leafed through the small stack absently mindedly. *'Imagine I haven't checked this thing since last Wednesday. I have really been out of it.'* Shaking her head she entered the elevator. It was already halfway up before she remembered to push the button for her floor.

With a shrug, she dismissed the few flyers and bills. A personal letter and an envelope with the hospital logo etched in the corner caught her attention. '*What now?*' Rosanna wondered. There was an uncomfortable feeling in the pit of her stomach, completely unlike what she felt a few minutes ago at the memory of Angus. This new feeling was accompanied by a mental sensation of disaster. She entered her condo in a daze.

'*Maybe they are going to fire me. Right now I don't know if I care.*' On that defiant note, she threw down the letters in one corner of the couch and hurled her body in the opposite direction.

Two hours later, Rosanna was still seated between the cushions dreamily staring into the carpet. Somehow the apartment felt barren and lonely.

'*Where was Angus?*'

The chair at his apartment was a haven. For a brief moment, she was sorry to have left his condo. At least his scent would be there to engage her senses. She longed to feel his arms wrapped around her again, instead of the pseudo memories which washed over her when she closed her eyes. The letters, the laundry, the call to her family, were all forgotten as she remained lost in thought.

'*I've got to get myself focused. This just won't do,*' she sighed. With a heavy heart, she headed towards the kitchen. Rosanna abandoned her dreams and faced the reality.

'*What do I really know of this man anyway? He seems nice enough. Can I be falling in love? It is possible so soon?*'

The questions tumbled one after the other as she went

through the motions of preparing some food. Her head ached. Giving up on what she was trying to do in the kitchen, Rosanna returned to the couch. The letter from the hospital caught her eye. Reconciled to dealing with its contents, she opened the envelope very slowly.

Dear Ms. Amadeo.

An appointment has been made for you on Monday June 10.

The Director of Nursing wishes to see you regarding a confidential matter.

If you are unable to keep this appointment, kindly notify the office at least 24 hours prior to rebook.

It was signed T. Tran for Ms. Barclay.

'Oh damn!' Suppose Angus is free for the day. It's too late to change anything now. I wonder why she wants to see me?'

A vision of the efficient looking nursing director was replaced by the face of Angus. *'He's all I want right now. I wish everyone else would just leave me alone.'*

Rosanna was having see-saw emotions. She realized that she was getting very strung up. The unusual activities of the weekend combined with the very real knowledge that she had slept with a man she barely knew were coming back to haunt her.

'Did he really care about me or was he just using me?'

She didn't know how to get in touch with Angus but she

needed to talk with someone. She knew her family was expecting her not only to call, but to come home as well.

'I'll call Mama and hope that everyone else is busy,' she decided. Her mother's commonsense approach to life was always calming if Rosanna could get past the reasons for not coming home.

She dialled the number and spoke rapidly in Italian.

'No Mama, I wanted to come but I was busy.'

'Busy? Too busy for your family?'

'No…I just had other things to do here.'

'Things? What things? Bring them home. We do it here. We don't see you too much you know.'

'I know but..'

'But! but! but! All the time 'but'. Rosanna…when you come home?'

'Hi Papa…next time I have a few days off I will come home.'

'You offa today Rosa. You no comin'? Yo Mama looka for you. Whatsa importante so mucha today?'

As usual, her father had taken over the phone. He switched to his own brand of broken English quite often to reprimand his children. He felt it saved his wife from being hurt by what he thought was her children's apparent indifference. Rosanna felt guilty. She knew that her parents expected her home. A vision of Angus rose before her eyes. She could feel the pull of his sexuality. The image of those amazing green eyes helped to break her lifelong habit of yielding to her father's not so subtle emotional blackmail.

'I'm sorry Papa. I told you I was busy. I met someone and we went out on a date. Next time I come down, I'll bring him to meet the family.'

There was no response to this shocking piece of news. Rosanna knew her father was dying to ask why she dated any man before the family met him. His continued silence spoke volumes.

'E Italiano?' he ground out after a significant pause.

'No Papa.'

'Ciao Rosanna'

The dial tone sounded loud in her ear. Rosanna shrugged and hung up the phone. Her father was shocked but not angry. He would call back after he had a chance to process the information. Long distance calls cost money. The usual practice at home was to discuss things with her brother Dominic. She shook her head laughing. She loved them dearly but their stifling chauvinistic values were too much. *I've fought Papa before for what I want. I will fight him for the right to love whoever I choose – Italian or not!'*

Rosanna was pretty sure, despite the emotional ups and downs, that she wanted Angus. He was everything a woman could ask for. So far he had shown kindness, patience and consideration. He was a wonderful lover. Rosanna could see the anger and arrogance, which was a part of him, but she had no fear of those qualities.

Over a light early supper she continued to dream about various aspects of their relationship, both real and make believe. By bedtime, she was beginning to doubt that the whole episode had, in fact, occurred. Angus hadn't called. *'Was he a figment of her imagination?'* Professionally, Rosanna knew that the resuscitation of a sick infant could take hours. She closed her mind to the nonsense of a phantom lover and opened it to the reality of a relationship with a busy doctor.

It was nearly midnight before the soft purr of the phone woke her up and she breathed huskily into the receiver.

'Hi Angus, how're doin?'

'I'm sorry Rosanna. I won't be able to see you tonight.'

'S'already tomorra. Babes ok?'

'No love, their condition is still very unstable and critical.'

'You can save them Angus. I know.….'

They both heard the urgent shout for his assistance and he quickly murmured 'got to go Rosanna. I love you.'

'I love you too.'

She was finally awake but knew that he probably hadn't heard her. Angus wasn't coming. *'Too bad!'* Her regret lasted as long as it took to turn over, but she smiled contentedly. Her lover was no phantom.

∞

Rosanna hummed contentedly as the prickles of water pounded her skin. The interview with her director sat at the back of her mind. *'I wonder if he'll call before I leave?'* Throughout the process of dressing and putting the final touches to her hair and makeup, Angus' face in the varying moods filled her conscious mind.

Ready at last, her final thought was not how she would appear to Mrs. Barclay, but whether Angus would find her attractive. The pink and navy trimmed lightweight linen coat dress looked professional and fit her ample curves to perfection. Navy sling back shoes and a matching purse completed the ensemble.

With one last imploring look at the telephone, Rosanna left her apartment. She tried with some difficulty to focus on the appointment and what was in store for her. Details were quickly pushed out of her mind to be replaced by a plan for the day that would include an evening with Angus. *'Perhaps a home cooked meal, for surely he would be tired, followed by some intimate time....before she had to go to work that night.'*

Rosanna's hand was actually turning the door knob, before she became consciously aware of arriving at the office of the director.

The cool green walls immediately reactivated the scent and feel of Angus. Rosanna knew she was completely out of tune with the importance of her surroundings. None-the-less she sat down gracefully in the seat offered, trying hard to focus on the face of Ms. Barclay.

'Ms Amadeo...Rosanna if I may?'

Rosanna shifted uncomfortably in the chair. *'Sure! Why not? We are all equal here Ms. Barclay.'* she thought saucily.

A questioning glance from the Director startled Rosanna. Her thought had seemed so real she felt that she had verbalized the impudent and totally inappropriate words.

She straightened up trying to look interested and intelligent. In reality all she really wanted to do was kiss…

'Ms. Amadeo…you seem tired. I'm sorry to have to get you up so early but I'm hoping that the news I have to give you will make a difference. Certainly the night work is a thing of the past.'

The last statement got Rosanna's attention quickly. Once again she straightened the pink and navy dress with nervous fingers giving her time to gather her wits together. A strained smile accompanied her next words.

'It is difficult at times. I'm usually asleep when I should be awake and…' a feeble gesture concluded the apology.

'Believe me, I do understand.'

The greying blonde hair, softly curled around the long rather aesthetic looking face, gave Ms. Barclay an angelic appearance. Rosanna knew it was quite at variance with a determined, strong willed character, often displayed when the director was fighting for the rights of her nurses.

'Now Rosanna, I have been going over your records and I am most impressed, both academically and clinically. There have been several glowing reports on your conduct, particularly in emergency situations.'

'Thank-you'

'I'm sure they are well deserved, however I didn't bring you here to discuss that aspect of your skills right now. These reports only added to my conviction that you would be….'

Rosanna tried hard to concentrate on the mouth as it opened

and closed on words like statistics, economics, good marks, committee…useful…audit..'

'What is she talking about?' sighed Rosanna inwardly. Giving up finally, she allowed her mind to drift to the hot tub as her head sank beneath the blissfully warm water, her lips glued to the man with the mesmerizing green eyes.

'Is that alright with you Rosanna?'

'Oh yes, perfectly,' she responded to a new position on the water bed.

'Take three more days off, dear. You can use your time to familiarize yourself with information for both jobs. The Standards and The Audit committee meet again on Thursday. It is vitally important, and I can't stress this enough, under no circumstances are you to have any contact with Dr. Mark Bailey or Dr. Angus Howard, until the investigation is complete.

For the first time since she entered the director's office to face this woman, who had single-handedly elevated the stature of the nurses here to a highly competent professional body, Rosanna felt deeply ashamed of her inattentiveness.

It seemed as if Ms. Barclay had not noticed anything strange, but something very important had been said long before she heard Angus' name.

'Oh dear God! What have I done? How can I make amends? She said she didn't want me to see Angus. How could she know about our weekend?'

The pause in the one sided conservation had become embarrassing. There was a discreet cough. 'Did you have any particular concerns or questions Rosanna?' There was a decided frown marring the features.

'Er...yes...I am naturally overwhelmed by the er...hon..er... confidence that you place in me.' She paused hopeful of a comment.

'As I said Rosanna, your marks, particularly in economics, were outstanding.'

No help there. The tone was becoming terse. Rosanna didn't know if she wanted to brazen it out any more. All she wanted to do was go home and be with Angus but Ms. Barclay' face registered more than just bewilderment. She could sense a disappointment bordering on displeasure and knew that her career could be on the line.

'I assume that I will get written confirmation of my appointment including all the duties expected of me?'

'Yes, my secretary Tuyet has everything ready for you in a sealed, confidential envelope.'

The frown had disappeared but the ready smile did not reappear.

'I must confess to being a little disappointed by your lack of enthusiasm. I'm rarely wrong in my judgment of people. You haven't something else in mind do you?'

'No, I am really excited about this opportunity, but I need some time to orient myself to the reality of big changes in my life. You said three days off, I believe?'

'Rosanna could almost see the sigh of relief and realized that she had behaved very badly indeed.

'It wasn't my intention to delve too deeply into the details surrounding your appointment right now. Most of the information is in the binder. I just wanted to assure myself that you would be able to hold your own, as it were, with the other members of the Audit committee. In the past, nursing representatives have been largely ignored or intimidated into leaving. You need time to prepare yourself mentally and play catch up with the information.'

Rosanna smiled warmly now. She was to be promoted to junior management with a seat on a hospital executive committee. The posts were highly sought positions. Being a part of the decision making process allowed nurses to have an impact on the policies and procedures which affect the running of the hospital. The committees comprised a mix of executive board members, managers, medical personnel and volunteers from the general public. Anyone seeking to move up the hospital corporate ladder could get a good start from this point.

The professional in Rosanna woke up like a bolt. There was plenty of time to combine love and a successful career. *'I must get my priorities right,'* Rosanna mentally chastised herself. She was as excited in that moment, as she should have been at the start of the interview. Too mortified to expose her mental lapse, she kept her composure with some effort, warming to the approving glance from the director. A slight chuckle puzzled Rosanna.

'You will be eminently good for that staid group of men my dear. We are often accused of being dinosaurs. Time for a little infusion of youth! I have no doubt that, academically, you will be able to hold your own.'

'Ms. Barclay?'

'I'm sorry. It's my turn to let my thoughts get ahead of me. I think we were discussing the night work.'

They weren't but Rosanna didn't contradict.

'When you initially applied here, we actually had to create a role for you so that we would not lose your considerable skills. You were clearly overqualified for the post of night supervisor but there was nothing else available. What I am about to tell you is in the strictest confidence. Our problem now, Rosanna, is that there have been some rather serious allegations made about the dispensation of government funds for research.'

'By members of our staff?'

'Members of the medical staff. We must do an internal audit on both our contributions to research as well as government grants. And, we must do it before any provincial or federal investigation. The hospital's reputation is also at stake. I know you will understand what the press will make of any hint that there has been a misuse of funding.'

Rosanna suddenly had a return of that sinking feeling. She knotted her fingers together. Angus! His name had been mentioned, but not in connection with their relationship.

'It isn't common knowledge around here but Colleen Mac Gregor is related to Angus Howard. I certainly trust your discretion but any hint of collusion between the auditors and the grant recipients could be disastrous for our long term research programs.'

'I understand.' Rosanna gulped hard, on a suddenly dry throat.

'Colleen is very proud of her nephew and his considerable

achievements. She will not sit back and allow any attack on his character or career.'

'I see.' Rosanna expelled her pent up breath.

'Any contact with her may impact directly on your impartiality. I am sorry that this seems to have come out of the blue but the committee's work is highly confidential. Before the board would approve your appointment, I had to ensure, not only your level of competence, but also your trustworthiness. '

'Ms. Barclay I feel that...'

'I understand your loyalty Rosanna but in any case, it is my opinion that your skills would be much better served in the nursing office on day duty. We have received an endowment to do some nursing research. The project I have in mind will help staff to understand and streamline their daily work load. I think that once you have had a chance to read the proposal, the research work, in your own field, will be very rewarding for you as well.

'Yes, yes, of course.'

'Rosanna, I'm only asking that you work with this group of men, using your skill and knowledge. Many of them are stubborn and set in their ways but it is important to get at the truth and preserve the reputation of the hospital.'

On that final note, Rosanna realized that the interview was over. Ms. Barclay stood extending her hand. There was a barely perceptible hesitation before Rosanna clasped it firmly. Whatever hopes she harboured for a relationship with Angus were decidedly put on hold.

Rosanna blocked any thoughts from her mind as she collected

the envelope and a large folder from Tuyet. Both felt like a death sentence in her hand. The envelope was quickly stored away in her purse and the folder tucked under her arm. The sunshine, so welcome before, was like a blinding light as she exited the side entrance of the hospital. Looking left and right, Rosanna picked up her pace, wanting to get home as quickly as possible.

The condo felt welcoming but there was no joy in Rosanna. Shoes were carelessly kicked in different directions. He body was flung into the couch with complete disregard for the effort it took to get herself ready for the interview. With nervous fingers Rosanna extracted the envelope from her purse. It fell quickly to the floor as the first of many harsh jangles from the direction of the telephone, sounded in her ears. With a pounding heart and nerveless fingers she stared at the phone, emotionally disconnecting from its seductive summons.

Chapter 9

'I can't answer it yet. I have to absorb this entire situation first,'
Rosanna realized. She was disconsolate. The full impact of
her promotion was sinking in. Aching eyes welled up with
tears, which soon found their way to the front of her dress.
She knew crying would not help. Impatient with herself, she
dashed them away and tore open the letter instead.

Dear Ms. Amadeo,

*We are pleased to offer you the position of Nursing Liaison with
concurrent roles on the Hospital Audit, and the Mortality and
Morbidity Committees. Your administrative tasks are outlined
separately and will be assigned from the Office of the Director
of Nursing.*

*Enclosed, please find the prospectus outlining the direction of
the Audit Committee, and the current issues to be addressed,
including your responsibilities.*

*Kindly read the enclosed literature and information. Your first
meeting will be held on June 14, at 9 am. The Mortality and
Morbidity Committee is on hiatus until September.*

Please sign the acceptance form and return same to nursing office..

If you have any questions or concerns, please do not hesitate to call me.

A Barclay RN MScN,PhD

The prospectus was several legal size pages in length and content. The phone rang two more times before Rosanna completed reading the material. It was a glorious opportunity and one that Rosanna would have been flattered to accept. The pleasure of accepting, in Ms. Barclay's office, fully cognizant of the enormity of prestige attached to it, was lost by her daydreaming about Angus. Rosanna shook her head fiercely, trying to banish the look and feel of him. She needed to think.

'I can't base my whole life on one weekend with a man who says he loves me. After all, Angus is 42 now, never been married…maybe he is not even the type to want any lasting commitment.'

As the thought came and went she knew it was unworthy. His very devotion to his sisters spoke volumes about his steadfast character.

'It doesn't mean anything' she argued internally. *'They are probably independent women who will only intrude as much as he will allow. A loving relationship needs so much more. Is he capable of sustaining that kind of relationship?'*

The arguments for and against were futile. She had already accepted the post by giving her word. Any relationship with him was out of the question. She knew that she would not even be able to explain why. Knowing it would not be forever didn't help. Rosanna had no idea if he would wait, trust her on faith alone or ….. ? She didn't even want to think beyond the moment and yet she could not avoid a final assessment of his probable response to her behaviour.

'Our relationship has been built on shifting sands. It won't hold when the tide of my rejection washes in,' she thought, profoundly disturbed by the possibility of a deep chasm of hurt on both sides of the issue.

Her previous experience with Derek played a great part in her summary. The young Australian doctor hadn't given a thought to how much pain he inflicted by his unannounced departure. She learned a hard lesson. Based on her own experience, Rosanna knew that she cared about Angus too deeply to ignore what it would mean to avoid any contact. Angus deserved better consideration from her, but she had no way of telling him the truth.

There was no optimism left in her. She knew Angus would be puzzled by her 'about face' behaviour. Rosanna could feel an unsettling cloud descending on her. In her usual way of arguing both sides she realized that if her work on the committee was helpful in getting him cleared it would pave the way for his valuable work to continue. She was left with a feeling of bitter consolation.

Rosanna did not sleep that night. She deliberately turned off the volume on the phone when the constant ringing actually began to generate signs of panic in her. The words, *'any involvement with Dr. Howard could jeopardize his…'* became a horrifying litany.

The phrase played over and over in her head until she finally screamed with frustration. In the end, it wasn't her thoughts which precipitated her flight from the condo. The mind could reason and accept but her body, kissed and caressed to distraction remembered his touch in every fibre of her being. Rosanna knew she needed, wanted, and craved more. She had to get away emotionally and physically. By sunrise, fatigue marking dark circles beneath the usually clear eyes, she hastily packed a small weekend bag and left by the back stairs. Tension had strung her nerves to fever pitch and she was sure Angus waited at every turn to berate her for making him look like a fool.

The drive from Toronto to Hamilton seemed twice as long as the usual forty five minutes, stress making her careless at times, but she knew her way well and pulled safely into the garage of her parent's home by 7:25 am. They would be up. Her mother never missed making breakfast for her father. She entered the split level four bedroom home using her key. The smell of espresso was welcome in the early morning.

The house was mercifully cool and she kicked off her shoes at the door before detouring through the carpeted living room arch to gaze, as she always did, at the brocade valance curtains, hanging from renaissance style windows. They were a thing of beauty. Her mother had decorated well, copying from an art book containing the styles of old Italy. The opulent looking area had been the envy of her friends, who often wondered how a carpenter could afford such luxuries.

In her youth, Rosanna never fully appreciated the enormous struggle her parents endured to create their beloved 'pais' within the home. Maturity had lessened the initial shame she felt when other friends had professional parents.

Rosanna's father had been abandoned as a child. He grew up in an orphanage run by nuns. His entire name had been manufactured by the Mother Superior at the Church. Antonio Castelo di Amadeo married Anna Palermo with little more than his carpenter's skills and a desire to do better. His choice of a wife, with just the right capability to compliment his own ambition, helped drive them to a new life and untold opportunities for their children. Growing up, each of them was always expected to be well-dressed, neat, clean and very polite. Indeed they were a constant source of pride to their parents.

'Rosanna! What are you doing here?'

'Rosanna, what's wrong?'

Both her parents had come into the living room, hearing the sound of the door and seeing no one. It was no surprise to find Rosanna. Without fail, she always stopped in the living room.

'I'm ok Mama, Papa.' She rarely spoke anything other than her parents' Italian dialect at home. Although she had studied Roman Italian at her father's insistence, it would have been a difficult conversation for them.

'I got three more days off so I decided to come home.'

'You look terrible Rosa. Something's wrong. I can see it.'

'I'm just tired Mama. I didn't sleep last night.'

'You worked?'

Rosanna didn't want to lie. Her mother would know, but she nodded affirmative just the same.

'You got here very quick Rosanna.'

'I left a bit early Papa.' She smiled warmly, trying to infuse a little truth to her words.

The strict but doting father, dismayed by Rosanna's continued spinsterhood, unabashedly adored his smart and beautiful eldest daughter. The proud father couldn't resist her smile any more than Angus. He would tell anyone about her at every opportunity but failed to realize that his daughter would have loved to be the recipient of his praise from time to time.

'I got a new job yesterday. It means a lot to me. No more night work.'

'That's good Rosa.' There was no excitement, just understated maternal pride. 'Time for you to go, Tonio.'

Anna, sensing a deeper discomfort in her daughter, shooed her husband off to work. She grabbed Rosanna's arm firmly and headed towards the kitchen.

'I'll make you breakfast. I can see you are not eating,' she announced hating to see the signs of fatigue visible in the dark circles beneath watery eyes. Tonio did not protest being excluded. He understood women's talk was important. Kissing his wife and daughter's cheek, he left quietly, knowing his Anna would get to the bottom of any trouble.

Much later, filled with sausages, eggs, fresh homemade bread, and a cup of delicious homemade coffee, Rosanna watched sleepily as her mother cleaned up. Anna's actions were purposeful. She would approach her daughter's problem in the same methodical way she did everything. It took very little time to return the kitchen to its normal pristine state.

Then and only then was Anna ready to tackle the issues troubling her daughter.

'You are not happy my child. You don't like this new job?' Anna sat opposite to Rosanna, sipping her own cup of coffee determined to understand her daughter's reason for lying.

'I do. It is a wonderful opportunity.'

'Then why are you not happy?'

There was no immediate response from Rosanna. She couldn't meet her mother's soft brown eyes, so like her own.

'Is it this man you met?'

Rosanna was startled.

'You think I don't know. All of you are the same. You think I don't know English.' The shrug which accompanied the words was pure Italian. 'I understand lots of things. I watch TV. I listen to radio. I don't have to speak English but I understand. Anyway my dear daughter, one look at your face tells me everything I need to know. Do you love him?'

Anna was not subtle. She left Sicily as a young teenager possessing very little formal education. She placed full trust in her slightly older husband to guide and support her. Hoping he would be a good provider, had been a chance she was willing to take on intuition alone. Despite his complete fidelity to family, Anna soon realized that raising five children, in a foreign land would require a strength she never imagined within herself. The early years of struggle taught her the value of being direct. She waited for her daughter's response, prepared to ask again if the truth was not forthcoming.

'Do I love him Mama? I think so, but I haven't known him for long.'

Wisely Anna did not ask the obvious. She had no wish to pry, but rather to get at the truth.

'So why is there a problem? I know he is not Italian but if you love him…?' she trailed off hopeful of a simple answer, something easy to fix. She prayed for any word which would take the shadows out of her daughter's face.

Rosanna held up a hand to forestall anymore probing. Anna's heart sank.

'My job is important Mama. I have already agreed to take it but it means…..it means… I can't see him anymore.' The tears held in check released themselves easily. The frustrating sobs which racked the body returned knowing that comforting arms were nearby.

'Not see him? For a job? What kind of job is this which separates love?' Anna inquired confused by the rules of today's world. Families might separate lovers, but not jobs. Even then, Anna would certainly not allow anyone to interfere with her daughter's happiness.

'What he does, Mama, is very important. He's a doctor.'

'Ah, very nice Rosa.' Anna interjected nodding approvingly.

'The government gives him money to learn about the things that make children sick. My job is to make sure he spends the money properly.' Rosanna's simple words were not meant to patronize. She knew that her mother was not sophisticated and lacked a wider understanding of the world. Terminology would confound her, but not simple logic.

'Rosa, this problem is just like marriage. Your father earns money. I spend it wisely.'

'I wish it were so easy.'

'It will be Rosa. You love him. He must be a good man. He will do the right thing and then you don't have to watch him anymore.'

She smiled at her mother's words of comfort. 'Easier said than done' she mumbled in English.

'Eh?'

'I thought you said you understood English Mama?' Rosanna teasingly held her mother's hand as she spoke.

'Just what I need to know.' There was finality to statement. They dropped the subject and went on to discuss other family issues.

'Are the kids coming over today?' Rosanna asked hoping to be able to catch up on some sleep.

'No. Tina is on holidays, so I am having a few days rest' Anna declared with a sigh of relief. She was referring to her daughter-in-law who brought the smallest children over during the day for babysitting. 'I don't know why Tina goes out. Dom makes enough money. She should stay home. I love to have the children here but they need their mother.'

Anna was a doting Nona and loved her grandchildren but she was just old fashioned enough to believe that mothers should be at home with their children.

'Things are different today Mama. A woman likes to know

she's making a contribution, helping her husband, having some independence.'

'Foolish girl! She would help more if she kept a nice house.'

It was a sore point, long since worked to death. Anna's ideas about a wife's responsibilities did not sit well with Tina. When Dominic had married Christina Marchese, the family was in awe of the pristine beauty who felt herself a cut above her in-laws. She had worn her virginity like a badge, letting everyone know that Domenic was getting the closest thing to the Madonna.

Her family, in Canada longer, had tried to give her the best education possible. She had been a poor student, barely completing high school before offering herself on the marriage market.

Her best accomplishment was a flawless Italian, which intimidated her fiancé's parents. Their simple Sicilian dialect was found wanting. The rift she created extended to her new siblings who found her 'stuck up.' Rosanna tolerated Tina's presence because of her brother but it was several years before the resentment wore down to be replaced by pity. Tina's lack of education was quickly evident when she was unable to match her husband's own university trained skills. She compensated by having four children in seven years. The children were welcome but the tactic backfired. There were no nannies to care for the growing brood and Tina was hopelessly overwhelmed and incompetent.

She pushed Dominic to get a better paying job as a corporate architect, but he steadfastly refused to leave his father's carpentry business. The technically gifted graduate used his skills to expand it, eventually creating an abundance of money for her. Tina held her peace but not her pride. After eleven years of marriage the gilt wore off. Tina floundered unable to mend the rifts she had created. The part time job was truly unnecessary, except to Tina's ego.

In her own heart, Rosanna knew that her mother was right. Tina was a born homemaker but pride and stubbornness had confused her values and she was unable to settle into any role that would compliment her home and family. Tina neglected the housework to stand on her feet six hours a day for minimum wages in a job she didn't need or enjoy. Rosanna's defence of her sister-in-law stemmed more from a need for self preservation than justice for Tina's actions.

In the early days before the rose coloured glasses came off, Tina had been held up as an example of the perfect Italian wife. Rosanna was firm in her resolve to succeed at a career but her ambitions had been driven further by the unfair comparison. She was determined to achieve more, and to be self supporting. Despite the history, she supported Tina's choice to be happy or not, depending on her own preferences, just as she herself had done. Rosanna refused to make it a point of conflict between her own values and those of her parents. The tension created rifts with her brother as well. Those fences were almost too high to be breached easily. Now, she just nodded and listened to her mother, but said little. It wasn't long before the effects of her restless night were taking effect.

'I need some sleep Mama. Is my room free?'

'Yes, of course. You are not married. This is still your home. I keep your room the same. I've told you many times.'

Rosanna accepted her mother's rebuke with good grace, kissing the soft cheek before heading down the hall. Two bedrooms had been added to the original structure and were elevated slightly. Rosanna's old room had been shared by her younger sister but after Dom married, Terry used his room until she eventually left home with her husband to live abroad. Like the rest of the house, the room was a thing of beauty, with cream colour eyelet curtains, complimenting the jade and peach tones in the bedspread and carpet.

Rosanna felt enveloped by the warmth and security of its very feminine appearance. The walls were decorated with pictures of her in lacy dresses for parties, first communion, graduations and all the milestones of a busy life. A cupboard hid boxes of old shoes and handbags. All the furniture had been hand made by her father. Neither of her parents had been impressed by the stark simplicity of the condo. She was suddenly aware that the side of her which used to love the frills was slowly fading to be replaced by a sterile clinical persona until…..

Rosanna stopped, quickly closing her mind firmly on the direction of her thoughts. She threw herself childishly on the mattress. A smile for the old Rosanna flitted across her lips before she turned over and slept.

Chapter 10

Angus was beside himself with anxiety. He knew there was no need. Rosanna had been a self supporting independent woman long before he turned up. She had a full life without him. He tried to rationalize her actions but failed to come up with an easy explanation for her unavailability.

He had called all day Monday, at regular intervals, but couldn't leave the hospital at any time during the 36 hours in which the skilled team worked on the very sick babies. Like everyone else, he had snatched a couple of hours sleep here and there in the on-call room but he needed to be within earshot if the infants destabilized suddenly. His hope that the boys did not share vital organs was doomed the minute he saw their tiny bodies. There was no way that immediate surgery would be possible. Their condition remained critical.

The phone was his only life line. Hope was fading fast as the ringing continued with hypnotic regularity each time he dialed the number.

'Damn Rosanna! Where are you?' he pleaded into the ringing phone. He continued to mutter nonsense to himself throughout Monday night. In exasperation, he vowed not to call again until he was free.

Despite his professionalism, Angus' mind was not 100% on his work. He spent time calculating when she should be at work Monday night. He hoped the unusual emergency might bring her to the unit. Her assessment of his character as 'a very private person' was accurate. It would prevent him from seeking her out, via his Aunt, until they were ready to acknowledge their relationship publicly. In his moments of need, he hoped that she would feel no such barrier and appear before his eyes. Her failure to either answer her phone, or materialize in person, frightened him.

His resolve to be circumspect wavered dangerously as he left the hospital at 3:30 am on Tuesday morning. He was even contemplating waiting for her outside her door but that seemed melodramatic. The idea was quickly abandoned.

Used to sleeping in fits and starts during an emergency, he knew he could rest for four hours then call her before she settled down for the day. He hoped she would be with him. Fatigue could not prevent a dreamy smile from lightening his face on the short drive home.

All his plans were doomed to disappointment. He overslept and the only call he received had been for his immediate return. Another crisis, another baby, another delay! His frustration mounted alarmingly causing a very unprofessional young nurse to make some inflammatory remarks which Angus wisely ignored. In his agitated state he thought it best to deal with distractions later.

It was after midnight again before he was able to leave the

hospital for the second time. Gaunt lines of fatigue etched his stony face. His eyes were pea green, bloodshot, and red rimmed, burning with the need for sleep, which he did, until Wednesday afternoon.

Wednesday evening, in desperation, he finally called his Aunt, when he knew she would be getting ready for work. The call itself wouldn't be unusual. Colleen had been working for over 10 years on night duty since the premature death of her husband. All the family members adjusted to calling at her convenience. She seemed distracted but responded well to her favourite nephew.

'Oh hello Gussie, I hear you've been very busy on Pediatrics.'

'Yes, we've had a couple of very unique touch and go cases. I haven't worked this vigorously for some time.'

'Why are ye calling Laddie? Is anything wrong?'

'No, I'm just tired and lonely and needed someone to talk to. You're my best girl, you know.'

'Angus, you are a young fool, wasting your life away on an old woman and I'm pretty sure you have said the same about your sister. You are not getting any younger. Morag and Megan don't need your help all the time anymore. It's time you made a life for yourself.'

'I'm aware of that but maybe I need them Aunty. The habits of childhood are so strong that it's difficult to change.'

'Buck up my boy. I worry about you.' Colleen's tone changed. She sensed a new, unfamiliar self-pity in the voice of her nephew.

'I'm fine' he lied. Then, as casually as he could, 'what's new with you?'

'Ach Laddie, my world is topsy turvy right now, but you don't want to hear about that.'

'Of course I do' he said, restraining his desire to beg with great difficulty.

'That Lacey's been on my back constantly. Just when I get into a routine with someone I have to adjust all over again. Lacey refuses to see my side of things. She complains endlessly. She's the most insipid girl, always sickly. I don't know how she's going to last. To be honest, I'd rather have Tilsma back than her.'

Colleen had launched into her tirade and hardly noticed the frightened silence on the other end of the phone.

'Gussie, are you listening? I knew you didn't want to hear.'

'No Colleen, I'm sorry, something distracted me for a moment. Did you say Annie was gone?' he improvised, knowing full well that she hadn't mentioned Annie at all.

Colleen knew too, but she interpreted his question as a balm to soothe her when he had been caught not paying attention.

'No, I didn't say Annie's gone. I said Lacey's back.'

'Aren't they the same thing?'

'No!' was the unequivocal reply. 'I liked Annie. I don't like Lacey.'

'Well, surely it's just temporary?'

'No Gussie. Lacey's been promoted to night supervisor, so I'll have to take my lumps with her or retire.'

'But Colleen....'

'No more now son. It's getting late and I have to finish getting ready. I'm off at the weekend. Come and have dinner with me.'

'I'll let you know Ok?'

Angus hung up the phone feeling depressed and anxious. His last call to Rosanna hadn't given him any indication that she didn't want to develop their relationship. She had been sleepy but she, as well as anyone understood the importance of his emergency call to the hospital. She had been so supportive of his work when they walked along the path at the children's playground. Perhaps he had been too forthright, sharing more than she wanted to know. It was obvious she was well mannered. *'Was she just being kind to me? Worse yet, pitying me?'*

Worried that he had told her too much too soon, he remained puzzled. He could not imagine that Rosanna would just ignore him. He wondered if he had frightened her off with his desire. *'Surely she would have told me to get lost, but she reciprocated in every way.'* The analysis of her character did little to comfort the shaken man. He had fallen deeply and quickly, exposing himself to the possibility of a big letdown. When she was in his arms it didn't seem possible but slowly, as the hours ticked away, the real possibility of a sham relationship loomed.

Fear and anxiety were dissipating to be replaced by a slow burning anger. Before long it turned into a red hot blinding rage, fed by guilt and pain.

∞

Rosanna paced endlessly in her room. She knew she had to return to town. She wanted to sleep in her own bed, hopeful that she could get an early start without worrying about rush hour traffic between Hamilton and Toronto. As usual, there was never a clear cut answer for her. The see-saw arguments so typical of her character plagued her all through the evening. She knew if she stayed, she could jeopardize her performance on the first day.

If she returned there was a real risk of seeing Angus. She would also have to deal with the ringing of the phone. She covered her ears hoping to stave off the imaginary ring and shut down the constant argument. In the end, she knew she could simply turn off her phone. She was no longer on call for the hospital. She had no idea how Angus would interpret her behaviour. Her disappearance was totally at variance with the persona of the woman who abandoned all reserve in his arms.

Gathering a few things together, she informed her parents of the decision.

'I'm going back to town. My new job starts tomorrow. I have to sort things out.'

'What things Rosanna? You have clothes here. You don't come too often. Why not stay? It's late.'

It was an argument she had heard many times.

'I'm going Papa.'

'That's Ok Rosa. You go. Your father just likes to have you close. You know that.'

Tonio gave his wife a surprised look. Normally she would back him up.

'Hush Tonio! Rosanna says she has things to do. Leave her alone.'

The stocky grey haired man was too bewildered to say more. Since Rosanna came home, his wife had been acting strange, very protective. He concluded it must be women's problems and kept his rather large nose out of it. He was sad to see his little angel leaving. Ignoring his wife's warning glance would not be worth the effort. She was fiercely protective right now. Instead he stood up meekly to accept Rosanna's farewell kisses. He slipped a $50 bill in her hand at the same time.

Rosanna didn't need money but her father needed to give it to her and she accepted his kindness with more kisses, grateful for his simple, gruff caring.

'I'll buy gas. Thanks Papa.'

Anna followed her out to the car, kissing and hugging the tormented child, created so much in her own image.

'Everything will come alright, Cara Mia. You see.'

In thirty-four years, her mother had never spoken English to Rosanna. The words fell off her tongue like a benediction and the daughter knew that her mother had practiced how to say the simple words of comfort clearly. Touched beyond belief by the guileless homily she received, Rosanna brightened a bit, knowing that oft times her mother's words were prophetic.

∞

It was after ten o'clock when the shiny late model ford pulled into the underground garage and its sole occupant tried to force herself from its cushiony confines. The fear, held in abeyance while she was miles away, returned. She sat still for quite a few minutes breathing deeply. Her head rested against the car seat.

'All I need to do, is to get through tonight. Once Angus becomes aware of the necessary audit, he'll understand my position. The first meeting would see the drafting of letters to the two parties involved. That should happen tomorrow then after that....'

She refused to dwell on *'after that'*. Rosanna made her way out of the car, locking the door securely and running head down to the elevator. Once inside she breathed a sigh of relief actually chastising herself for the nonsensical way she was behaving. Pushing the button she concluded that they were both civilized people, able to deal rationally with the impasse.

∞

Even when Angus was gripping her shoulder, his eyes narrowed slits, nostrils flaring, Rosanna did not actually believe it was him. Her ride up in the elevator had been interrupted at the ground floor. The first person waiting to get on was the last person she wanted to see.

She was held speechless by the look of blinding fury on his face. He warned her not to say a word. He spoke tightly and softly for the benefit of the other passenger who looked to be as high on drugs as Angus was on rage.

Of the two men, Rosanna would have preferred to take her chances with the stoned youth who looked benign, than the man whose eyes resembled a hurricane swept Caribbean sea.

'Angus I….I…'

'Not now!'

She subsided quickly giving him no reason to feel more justified in his actions. She found her keys easily, but the lock kept sliding away from her nervous fingers. Impatient and ready to burst with the ferocity of his feelings, Angus grabbed the key and deftly opened the door, dragging them both inside.

'Angus you have no right to treat me like this….I don't deserve what you are doing.'

'Deserve? You deserve nothing but my contempt. I thought you were decent. I thought you cared. The role reversal of today works well for you eh? Love 'em and leave 'em used to be a man's prerogative. I never subscribed to that. Maybe I should have.'

Rosanna felt his pain to her very toes, aching inside, knowing what she had caused. She was tense with nerves. It was a struggle to hold them in check. All she knew was that she wanted to kiss the hurt away. She backed away from the riveting words, pouring like icy venom from his mouth. She put her hands over her ears to stop the sound. Unable to remain stoic in the face of his pain, tears began flowing freely.

'Angus please?' Any words she uttered, seemed to inflame him more. He removed the hands from her ears.

'Please? Please what? Make love to me, go away, stop shouting? Please what Rosanna? Three days! Not a word…no messages…nothing but that damn phone ringing endlessly.' His voice had gone dangerously soft. 'Please what Rosanna? I told you if it pleases you, I would do it. I meant what I said.'

Rosanna raised her eyes to stare at him. Her own were filled with shock and pain. There was no justification in the world for hurting him the way she had. *'He's here now. Who's to know? Who would ever have known? I could have relied on his discretion. Was it too late?'* She widened her eyes hopeful that she could see something reassuring in his. She couldn't be sure.

'Angus, I'm sorry. I never meant to hurt you. Please believe that.'

'I believe it!'

'Circumstances …er… things happened that….that…'. Lips trembling, she still couldn't explain. It seemed futile to try. Despite his words there was a look of weary resignation on his face, a stillness that was deceptive. *'What did it mean?'* she thought.

'Angus?' Her voice was a whisper.

She could say no more for he pulled her to him wordlessly holding her close, apparently entranced by the full lips. Almost against his will it seemed, he cupped her face, kissing her fiercely. She sobbed in his embrace praying that he could see in her expression, in her response, what words couldn't explain. He was still very angry. She could feel it in the arms which wrapped themselves around her trembling body. He kissed her again, forcing her lips apart thrusting his tongue within her mouth, punishing even as he sought the warm crevices.

The non-verbal onslaught continued as his mouth left blazing tails of white heat down the length of her neck. His movements continued to the barrier of her blouse, pulling at the fabric impatiently tearing away the buttons in his eagerness to capture the breasts still bound by the lacy black fabric.

She didn't stop him. She realized the extent of his need, driven by her own desire. She revelled in his dominance, feeling secure that he would not hurt her. She had backed her way to the couch. The ridge of it was pressing painfully into her low back.

The force of Angus in front of her bent her away from him. She was in danger of falling over but he held her firmly with one hand while the other quickly disposed of the confining harness. Once exposed, his eyes changed. His head bent forward to blaze a trail of heat from her neck, beyond the soft rise to the firm tips. Rosanna felt her body change with his touch. She clutched at him, holding the golden hair like a life line.

She knew Angus was deeply aroused. His firm pulsating length, pressed tautly at her hips, charging her with shock waves of desire. It wasn't long before the shapely legs parted invitingly, giving access to his still confined need. She grasped fiercely at his head, threading her now nerveless fingers through the silky strands. Angus gripped her hard with one arm, but they were falling. The free hand left her tender breasts to undo the button on her pants. They slid down her hips, as gravity got the better of her now unprotected torso. With hardly a conscious action, she found herself naked in the cushiony depths of the couch, Angus towering above her.

There was no force or violence, just an impassioned assault on her senses. Angus was still clothed in casual shorts and an open neck shirt. He made no move to undress except for his shoes. Rosanna was about to question him when he literally threw himself on her attacking the already bruised and aching mouth. He didn't stop long, but alternatively kissed and licked the gleaming skin until Rosanna was moaning and rocking with need. Her toes dug dangerously into the soft fabric at her feet.

She couldn't take much more and moaned piteously, spewing out words in the dialect of her parents. She almost lost total control when she felt his warm breath stirring the hair already parted by the probing fingers. She called out again as the hot kisses he planted in her garden of womanly softness soon sent the unbearable agony, the delicious sweetness, soaring upwards, filling her.

Rosanna's writhing body begged for total fulfillment. Her mind did not register anything except the feel of Angus as he entered her with one hard stroke. She uttered breathless unintelligible words, head flying from side to side unable to articulate coherently, feeling only the strong vigorous assault so different from before but equally welcome.

Rosanna peaked several times before the driving onslaught ceased suddenly, leaving her satiated body limp with perfect contentment. Suddenly Angus was speaking for the first time since he kissed her.

'Thanks for a wonderful time Rosanna, but I have to go.'

Her eyes opened wide, the colour almost gold in the aftermath of the glow created by this wonderful man.

'Go Angus? I don't understand.'

'I think you do. You used me. I used you. The mutual gratification of our generation! Good bye Rosanna.'

Long before the words sank in and she was able to sit up, he was gone.

Chapter 11

'Good morning Ms. Amadeo. Welcome to the committee. Gentlemen, would you kindly introduce yourselves?'

As the curious eyes of each member met hers in a nod of welcome, Rosanna listened carefully matching the faces to the names she had memorized. She held herself rigidly, not in fear but in a white hot anger that would have matched and surpassed that of Angus.

'Gentlemen, and..er.. Lady' began the chairman calling the meeting to order. 'Our purpose in meeting here today has been clearly mandated in the prospectus you should have received last week.' The monotonous voice droned on for some time before he paused to take questions or comments.

'Mr. Chair, may I suggest that since I'm the only female on this committee, your address be directed to 'members' instead of 'gentlemen and lady. I have no need to be identified separately.' A stunned silence followed the suggestion. It was clear that no one expected her to talk. The chairman looked around in silent query. There were 'ayes' all around in response to this.

Rosanna settled back, having made her point. She waited to see which subcommittee she would be asked to join. As expected, medically skilled practitioners would sort through the data of findings and clinical procedures. The members familiar with accounting would delve into the budgeting and accounting aspects.

Rosanna hoped they would deal with Dr. Bailey, first but Angus' project headed the agenda.

Each member was expected to devote at least an hour daily to complete the audit before the three month deadline was over. To her relief and the only bright spot in the meeting was that the notification letters to the primary grant recipients would be delayed for one week before posting. She needed time to settle her assaulted senses before seeing Angus again. The meeting was adjourned on time allowing each subcommittee one hour to plan their own strategy for working together.

Dr. Rosenthal and Dr. Pappas, who were going to collaborate with Rosanna, appeared to be amiable men, glad of the opportunity to work with so beautiful a colleague. She quickly disabused them of any notions they might harbor about a light flirtation. It was done with just the right touch of firm assertiveness which left the trio smiling comfortably.

The balance of the day was spent in the nursing office, doing some research on statistics for Ms. Barclay. It wasn't so heady or exciting as the night supervisor's job but it kept Rosanna on a steady plodding pace necessary for her inner self to heal. Angus had splintered that fragile tenuous link with the very feminine side of her. A mere spark would leave it in ashes.

She held herself responsible as much as he. That admission alone forced her injured pride to return to work Thursday morning. Once the meeting was over, Rosanna could do little more than smile and function like a robot outside of the boardroom. That night, tears of shame and humiliation flooded her pillow. She didn't cook, preferring to pick up a salad at the deli. She neither called any of her few acquaintances nor family members.

Being a new face around the hospital on the following day, she remained polite but distant to any overtures. The 9-5 hours precluded the possibility of meeting Colleen Mac Gregor. Rosanna needed time and she got it but the weekend loomed in front of her like a gaping hole ready to swallow up her fragile nerves.

∞

On Friday night, exhaustion and uncertainty threatened to choke her. Those first two days she had been able to maintain the façade of a professional woman, dedicated to her job. By the end of the following week, she seriously began to question the wisdom of accepting a job which had put a budding relationship in deep, and likely irreversible, jeopardy. The truth, when admitted, left her feeling so bereft. Rosanna knew that some of the events were outside her control but her own behaviour left a lot to be desired. With no further word from Angus, what he thought of her, was abundantly clear.

In the cold light of day, Rosanna searched for reasons why she had run away, instead of facing Angus like an adult, but answers eluded her. Part of her psyche understood that she would do absolutely nothing to endanger his work. There was no doubt in her mind that something was amiss with the whole concept of an audit. No man, who came with such a deep love of his family, and dedication to his work, could possibly do anything to sabotage the investigative nature of his research. Rosanna could sense and know his commitment.

As she lay in bed, tears ebbing and flowing in her heart before escaping like an unstoppable river from her eyes, the disheartened woman knew that her fragile feminine nature was unable to withstand much more without help. The thought of going home crossed her mind. Her mother's gentle care and warmth would be just the comfort for her troubled soul. The last trip home had worked wonders. Parents rarely found their children wanting. To return so soon would surely signal, to her deeply sensitive parent, that there was still no satisfactory resolution to her problems. Rosanna didn't know if she wanted to trade off her mother's anxiety for a few hours of balm to her soul.

It didn't take long for her to realize that it would be impossible to hold on without help. *'I have no genuine, established friends to call. What kind of a life am I living? I am so isolated from everything. Was it my choice?'* The lack of a deep and sustaining friendship was something Rosanna chose not to explore. Her siblings had always provided the help and support she needed but growing up between two boys was quite different. Her younger sister Terry, was one of twins and therefore closer to her male womb mate than an older sister. Indeed, the more Rosanna delved into her actions, the more she realized how her self- imposed isolation from an active and full social life evolved as part of the need to be a support to her family. She spent so much time helping her mother negotiate the language needs of living in a non Italian community that having fun was strictly limited to the religious holidays.

Even as the thought came and went, she remembered the day, standing at the fence in the playground with Angus. Watching the children reminded her of the all the times she felt left out of social activities because her mother needed the child's voice to articulate and translate adult themes. It hurt that a good deal of her life had been spent acting as a surrogate for her mother's limited role outside the home. And yet, she could not consider herself unlucky. All their basic needs of food, warmth, shelter and love were fulfilled in abundance.

Rosanna rose from the bed and went to the bathroom to splash cold water on her puffy, tear stained face. It was no use. Even as the cold water seemed to freeze her emotions, more tears threatened. Leaning over the bathroom sink, she struggled to rein in her emotions. A trip home was definitely necessary.

∞

An hour later, Anna greeted her weary daughter with all the love she could muster from her giving heart. Warm food, hugs and kisses did much to take the sting out of a week in which Rosanna felt as if she was pushed to her emotional limit. Her sense of self was teetering on the edge of oblivion.

Safe at last in the room of her childhood dreams, and propped up in bed, the drained and deeply unhappy woman held on to the cup of warm tea that her mother brought into the room. Anna did not ask a lot of questions. She sensed the need to be quiet and wait. It was clear that her daughter was suffering greatly. Beyond providing comforting arms and a soothing voice, she could do little. The sadness wasn't about work. No job could bring such tears. Even Anna knew that her child's heart was breaking over a man. *'How could he not love this child of hers?'* She felt anger well up inside. Like all sensitive mothers she sat at the bedside, watching as Rosanna finished the tea, and settled down to sleep. She hummed a familiar, simple nursery tune and waited until the sobs subsided into deep even breaths before turning out the light and leaving the room, with footsteps as heavy as her heart.

∞

Rosanna knew her mother had added some special herbs to ensure a good night's rest. In the light of day, she felt rested and less emotional, but the quandary of Angus remained. For a long while she lay in bed, looking around her room. The adult mind compared the young woman who gave up the comfort and safety of her parent's home for adventures abroad. That had nearly been a disaster too. Now, she was a certified spinster, still trying to prove that she could be independent, even as she allowed a man to once again complicate her life. *'But Angus felt different'*. Unfortunately, her rationale could not hold up under intense self scrutiny.

Tired of the endless and useless thoughts, she forced herself out of bed. It was well past breakfast time. Surprised that her mother hadn't called, she washed and made her way to the kitchen, the smell of fresh coffee drawing her like a beacon. Anna was busy at the stove. Rosanna went over and kissed her mother's soft cheek, whispering a loving thank you. She hardly had time to utter another word, before the front door opened and her older brother Dominic came in.

'No use in frowning at me in that way. Ma called me last night. Now I can see why.'

Her bulky, adorable, older brother held out his arms for a hug. He was such a welcome sight. Try as she might, she could resurrect no anger or rancour towards her mother for calling in reinforcements. It was the way of things.

'Don't you have anything better to do today, Dom?'

'Truth is Sis, I'm on my own. Tina took the kids to Nona Marchese and Dad is working on a project with Jacks and Vito.'

'Is everything alright?'

'Yeah, Tina's been upset lately. You know her mother will spoil her for the day and take care of the kids.'

'Same with me, except I don't have kids.'

'Aw c'mon Sis. You know it's different with you.' He looked up smiling, in that angelic way of his, when Anna placed a cup of coffee in front of him. 'Thanks Ma.'

'*Nothing ever changes*', Rosanna thought. Standing there in the kitchen watching her brother interact with their mother was just like stepping back in time. She felt no resentment that he had been spared the tasks she had when they were children. Culturally, that was just the way they evolved. Dominic would be petted and pampered. Rosanna would be expected to follow suite, waiting on her male siblings hand and foot. She had no doubt that part of her brother's willingness to come home was due to the need to be coddled by his mother, or so she thought. His next words surprised her.

'Hey Sis, I want to show you something. Do you have time today?'

'I'm not doing anything special, but I did come home to be with Mama.'

'She won't mind….. will you Ma?' he questioned, giving an even more saintly and irresistible smile in his mother's direction.

Anna nodded, good naturedly, and soon shooed her two children out the door. Despite being taken aback by his odd behaviour, Rosanna held her tongue. Dominic was acting in a strangely different manner. He took his astonished sister out for a late brunch at a decidedly un-Italian, but well kept restaurant. Mostly, the conversation was light-hearted. Rosanna wanted to get caught up on the antics of her nieces and nephews. Her brother had a good sense of humor and soon had her laughing. The meal was hardly done when he rose from the table.

'Where are you taking me?' she questioned as he pulled her, towards his large late model truck.

'You'll see. Just sit and enjoy the ride.'

And she did. Dominic took her on a roundabout route to Niagara Falls, a short distance from her family home in Hamilton. The truck ate up the miles easily. He played some country and western music, so culturally different from his heritage. The twangy sound of guitars blared out of enormous speakers. Rosanna knew that growing up her brother had been caught up in Country style music, although he didn't let his parents know. After the spaghetti western movies came out, none of his peers questioned his right to be a part of that culture. Clint Eastwood was Dom's hero.

Her brother drove until he found a spot which had been a secret 'get away' place for them as kids. After purchasing his first car, he had taken his sister on a drive which included the falls and surrounding areas. They loved the Dufferin Islands just west of the famous Niagara Falls. Whenever they needed time alone, this was where they came, but it had been years since their last visit. Rosanna recalled that time, when her brother disclosed his desire to propose to Christina Marchese. Rosanna wasn't happy but she supported his decision. They did not come back again.

Dominic parked the car and got out, encouraging his sister to join him. Although heavy set, he was light on his feet and remarkably fit.

'You remember the first time we came here don't you?'

Rosanna nodded, moved to rediscover this side of her brother. 'You just bought your first car. It was a sunny day, a lot like today and you were as nervous as hell about going to university in the fall.'

'Good memory. You were really nice to me on that day but then, you've always been able to cheer up anyone. I suppose that's why you got into nursing?'

'Not really, although I like it now. It's just that Dad wouldn't let me do anything else. I never told you Dom, but I wanted to be an economist.'

'You surprise me! Bay St. dreams?' Dominic shook his head puzzled by this view of his sister.

'Once upon a time I had those dreams, but I am as close to Bay St. as I'm going to get right now,' she responded derisively. The siblings laughed. The location of Rosanna's work place and condominium, each bordered the famed financial district which included the Toronto Stock Exchange.

They continued to reminisce about their childhood, while walking along the water's edge, crossing the bridges and traversing the pathways. It was sometime before Dominic got serious.

'I know you thought that I came home today because I wanted to be spoiled, but when Ma called me last night she sounded very worried. I asked Tina to spend the day with her mother. Ma's upset about you Sis. What's goin' on?'

It was Rosanna's turn to be surprised. Her brother had never really been interested in what she was doing beyond a surface inquiry. He was clearly busy with his own family and helping his father expand the business. He would be the last person she expected to find as a confidant.

'I don't know what to say Dom. I got a new job. I like it, but it conflicts with a relationship I was…..'

Rosanna trailed off. Giving her brother intimate details would only generate anger in him. She didn't want him tracking down Angus with a shotgun.

'Why can't you talk about it? Is there some secret?'

'Well yes and no, but it's hard for Mama to understand. I don't understand it myself.'

'Look Sanny,' he said gently, holding her shoulders and using her childhood nickname, 'I am sure Ma would be upset at first but she will get over it. I'll talk to Dad…. bring him around.'

'No! No! Dom. It isn't that easy.'

'Yes it is. Doesn't matter who you love. Ma just doesn't want you to be unhappy anymore and now that I've seen you for myself, I understand what she was worried about.' He paused staring at the ground before continuing. 'Look, bring her home. We'll sort things out.'

'What did you say?'

'Sanny, it's ok. Bring her home. I've figured it out already and I'm ok with it.'

Rather than a grateful hug, Dominic was surprised to see his sister giggle, then laugh until tears ran down her face. 'Is that what you think? You think I'm a lesbian?'

'Well, you know, you're thirty four, not married. Every time I set you up with some guy you brush him off. The last guy said you wouldn't even let him kiss you goodnight. He told me you were a lesbian.'

'What? Oh Dom. You always find the same type of self centered guy who thinks I should be so grateful for his attention. They just don't appeal to me. No, I can assure you I am not a lesbian, although facing that might be easier that what's happening now. I think I love him, Dom. No in fact I know I do. The problem is really work related. My new job is to audit his work. We can't even be friends.'

'You won't be auditing him forever. When it's over? What then?'

'He'll hate me for what I've done.'

Gathering her in his arms Dominic held on tight. 'Oh Sanny, I would kill him for hating you.'

'Thanks Dom and now you sound like the mafia. Be serious.

He's an adult and so am I. I'm touched that you cared enough to give up this time for me, but really, there's nothing to be done except play out the game 'til the end, no matter how much it hurts.'

The knitted brows said a lot about her brother's genuine concern. 'If it gets too bad will you call me?'

She answered him with a long look, which spoke volumes. 'Ok, ok,' he said, raising his hands in mock surrender. 'I'll leave the gun at home.'

They returned to Hamilton with reassuring smiles. Rosanna didn't go on to explain much more about Angus than what she had said at the small islands but Dom had a clearer picture of her new job. He was proud of his sister and told her so. Warmed by the time and attention devoted to her, Rosanna felt confident enough to return to Toronto. She assured her mother that she was not angered by the sibling intervention. She hoped the courage would last into the coming week. Feeling less intimidated by the upcoming challenge to her resolve, she drove back to Toronto late in the evening. The Sunday was spent reviewing her materials, checking facts and numbers and bolstering her resolve, all actions designed to generate courage. She needed a quiet undemanding day at home, to prepare herself for weeks ahead.

Chapter 12

The second meeting of the committee was a severe test of her composure. The letter was drafted to Angus, informing him of the decision to audit. As the meeting progressed, Rosanna felt a growing sense of disquiet. She hated allowing her emotions to show, but found it difficult to prevent fleeting glimpses of anger to dance across her face.

'Are you in disagreement with the wording of the letter Ms. Amadeo?'

'I wasn't aware that I had made any comment, Mr. Chairman.'

The stout gentleman bristled a bit at her tone then went on to explain, 'I thought I noted a frown.'

'Please don't read anything into the way I look. I can assure you that I will verbalize any concerns I have.'

She hoped she wouldn't have to make a statement each meeting. So far the other members treated her with respect, but there had been a touch of condescension creeping into the tone of the day's procedures and her nerves were raw with the sound of Angus' name being constantly repeated.

Rosanna was a complete professional. Despite much inner turmoil, her tone remained within the bounds of correct behaviour. The chairman accepted her rebuke with some surprise, not missing either point. He nodded respectfully, showing some admiration for her absolute determination to hold her own equally with the other members. Rosanna also knew he would not forget what she said.

The chair concluded the session, letting everyone know that Dr. Howard would be coming to the next meeting to be apprised of the manner in which the investigation would proceed. All committee members were expected to be in attendance. Stressing the importance of being prepared to question the Doctor intensively, he pushed a fist in the air as if preparing himself for a fight. Rosanna was hard pressed not to laugh. Much of his bluster made him look more like a Prima Dona. Rosanna had seen it before in her Father and many men of his generation. She knew the real power at home was her mother. Curious about the connection, she wondered who was pulling the strings behind this man.

Mr. Humphreys ask the recording secretary to ensure that Dr. Howard receive an outline of the information which would be needed. Satisfied that he had everyone on board with what Rosanna perceived to be a vendetta, the chairman smiled. Rosanna felt a chill run down her spine. There was no warmth in his eyes. Wondering at the process, the lone female member raised her hand.

'Mr. Chairman, how much will we be able to rely on the information, received from the grant recipients, for clarification?'

'That depends, Ms. Amadeo. Some grant recipients jealously guard their work. The possibility of theft of information can be damaging to years of work. Others may be eager to assist. I often find this is used to cover the very discrepancies these committees need to discover. From what I have heard of Dr. Howard, he's a young…er…man who will be unlikely to cooperate.'

Rosanna noted the slight hesitation and the tone which followed. It was full of innuendo. Her brows raised a fraction, followed by a narrowing of her eyes. '*What unmitigated gall!*' she thought defending in her own mind the man she had picked to pieces herself since morning. The chairman's prejudice was not a benign issue. Even if the allegations were true, it had no bearing whatever on Angus' conduct with respect to his work.

The chairman tried to stare down Rosanna but hastily closed his half open mouth when she returned his gaze unwaveringly. He had no further wish to be reprimanded. 'It there is nothing else….? His close-set pale blue eyes circled the room avoiding a pair of frosty brown ones. As there were no further questions, he adjourned the meeting.

Rosanna was thoughtful for the balance of the day. Whatever occurred between her and Angus personally, it paled beside her fury with narrow minded people in position of authority. There was little she could do of course. The inner defense brought out all of her mothering instincts. She wanted to protect him. Hot on the heels of that thought came a burgeoning need for him, for his body, for his warmth and love. The papers she had been looking over, blurred. She was grateful that no one else could fit in her small office space. Rosanna knew she had been a total emotional disaster, teetering between love and hate, prosecution and defense. *'That man has me so tied up in knots',* she acknowledged.

For the first time since she sat in Ms Barclay's office more than three weeks ago, Rosanna felt the need of company. Leaving her small cubby hole, she went out into the main area where all the nursing supervisory personnel had small offices. The support staff shared a larger area which had been partitioned off to give the more senior secretaries a certain amount of privacy. It reminded her of the principal's office in high school.

She made her way over to Tuyet Tran, Ms. Barclays's efficient Vietnamese-Canadian secretary. The young woman had been brought over to Canada as a young orphaned teenager on one of the many life and death boat trips during the late 70's and early 80's. Her struggle for survival had been much admired. She publically offered deep gratitude to the anonymous family who fostered her and credited them with giving her a life altering opportunity.

Following a few years of service in the secretarial pool, the appointment as executive secretary to the director of nursing came as a surprise to no one. Tuyet was competent, efficient, and discreet. She was also a constant reminder to those less ambitious that there is no excuse for failing to realize goals however big or small. Rosanna had been awed by the story when she first came to the hospital and spoke briefly with her then. There had been little communication until Rosanna's appointment. Tuyet had given her the envelope after the interview with a smile and a word of congratulations.

Of all the people who Rosanna avoided this past week, Tuyet was not one. There was a quiet strength and aura of peacefulness about her which Rosanna could not ignore.

She paused by Tuyet's desk for a few minutes each day to exchange pleasantries. It was the neat, well kept walnut desk with the fresh flowers perched on the corner that Rosanna slowly made her way.

'Hi Rosanna! Are the stats getting on your nerves?'

'Can you tell?'

'I've seen that look before. What you need is a break. I'm just going down to the cafeteria. Would you like to join me for a cup of tea?' Her head was tilted to one side, eyes bright in an irresistible gesture of welcome. It was impossible to refuse.

'Ok Tuyet. You and my mother believe tea cures everything but you need to know I'm a coffee girl.'

Tuyet laughed. 'Your mother sounds like a wise woman.'

There wasn't much difference in the height of the two women. Rosanna wore low heeled comfortable shoes and Tuyet wore high heels which gave her shapely calves and trim figure a nice balance. Her leaf green suit was neat and business like.

The large cafeteria was near empty at mid afternoon. It was change of shift for nursing and maintenance staff. Most people were scurrying to finish their tasks, then hand over to the incoming shift. The pair found a window seat and talked amiably while sipping the hot fragrant chamomile brew.

'Good for the nerves' advised Tuyet to the almost exclusive coffee drinker. 'How's the committee going Rosanna?'

There was no hesitation regarding discretion. Rosanna was required to prepare a summary of the meeting to be presented to Ms. Barclay each Friday. Her own portfolio would hold observations not included in the meeting minutes. Tuyet was the one who typed up Rosanna's handwritten notes. The question was more than perfunctory. She was interested in Rosanna's own personal observations.

'Tuyet, do you know Dr. Howard?' Rosanna blurted out the question without thought.

'Why do you ask Rosanna? I can't answer your question directly but I do want to be honest with you.'

Tuyet's answer was puzzling. *'What on earth did she mean?'* Rosanna thought. She stared into the dark almond eyes. 'I don't want to put you on the spot Tuyet. If there is a reason why you can't say anything, I'll understand. There's certainly been enough secrecy around this already.'

The truth of the matter was simply that Rosanna longed to discuss him with someone…anyone who was not getting ready to pick his career to pieces. She longed to see him, knew it was impossible but would have been glad to hear some compliments. The silence between the women lengthened until Rosanna was seriously contemplating coming in early to 'run into' Colleen hoping for some news. A wholly Italian shrug of the shoulders seemed to release something in her companion

'He's my foster brother Rosanna.' Tuyet's words fell into the silence.

'Huh?... He's what!?'

'Oh yes, Angus has women relatives all over the place.' Clearly Tuyet felt a need to release her own concerns.

'You better explain Tuyet and you have my absolute word it will go no further.'

'It has been difficult for me but Ms. Barclay trusts me implicitly. I worked hard to gain that trust. Since the committee is underway, Angus and I will be incommunicado until its work is done.

'I'd like to hear the story Tuyet. We'll be friends only, talking, nothing more.'

'Ok Rosanna, why don't we meet for supper after work? We can get some Vietnamese food and eat undisturbed in my cousin's restaurant.'

'Just name the time and place.'

Rosanna's hands began to tremble. Here was yet another side of Angus to be seen. She could listen to her heart's content. She dared not reveal her own involvement. Tuyet saw her as someone to trust. It was critically important not to let her down. Rosanna had no doubt that Angus would not have shared information about their weekend tryst with anyone.

The Saigon Palace was a busy cafeteria style restaurant off the beaten track but close enough to Chinatown. One didn't need to guess at the cuisine from the name. Everything else was strictly 'Broadway', with the garish neon signs and large food posters. There were a few potted plants, tables covered with plastic, lined up against the walls. It was well used and busy, but scrupulously clean. Tuyet and her guest were seated at the best table by the store's front window. Huong bowed graciously welcoming his much admired cousin and her friend.

They were given an unlimited array of dishes to choose

from. Rosanna was surprised by the hot spicy taste of the food, distinctly different from the Chinese fare she had shared with Angus.

'We'll talk after we eat. I want your mind and body to enjoy the food.' Tuyet smiled before directing her attention to the plates filling the table. She offered each one to Rosanna encouraging her to try a little of everything.

Later, replete from the marvelous selection of foods, served with flaky white rice and cup after cup of Jasmine tea, they spoke.

'Someday, I will return the favor in an Italian restaurant Tuyet. This meal was not only delicious but exciting too.'

'My thanks, for your compliments. I will pass them on to my cousin.'

'Has he been here long?'

'No, only about six years. We are the only survivors in the family. My mother and his father were brother and sister.'

Rosanna who understood the importance of family nodded sympathetically.

'You are a kind person Rosanna. Very easy to talk with… very understanding.'

'Thank you, I'd like to think that I have even a small measure of those qualities Tuyet. But don't make me out to be something I am not.'

'The Vietnamese place much value on the aesthetic side of people. Manner and proper address are a very important part of our culture.'

'You have a reason for telling me that don't you?'

'Even though I have spoken with you many times, I have never been sure if your professional face matched your personal face. Please don't be offended but I have seen many of the two faced kinds of people. It's difficult to know which side, if any, merits trust.'

'That's a universal problem Tuyet.'

'Yes. I understand. In our culture, we do not condone bad manners. Therefore people with unacceptable behaviour are ostracized from social gatherings.'

Rosanna was still not sure of the point the Vietnamese Canadian girl was trying to make. *'Is she talking about me or herself?'* she wondered.

'Don't try to understand me or my thought process Rosanna. I'm afraid that there is enough of each environment in me to engage in mindless emotional warfare, common in children raised in a cross-cultural home.'

'I may understand better than you think.' Rosanna smiled realizing that the cautious demeanour was a way of protecting herself from being misinterpreted. 'My own upbringing has been a mixture of two cultures. Probably, I have not had nearly the same degree of difficulty that you experienced but I often find myself at odds with the very strict Italian expectations of my parents meeting head on with the freer less confining North American lifestyle. I'm neither fish nor fowl, but merely a unique product of both worlds.'

Tuyet nodded sagely. She weighed the words carefully before speaking again.

'You know Rosanna, you sounded just like Angus when

you spoke. He has often tried to get me to quit trying to be anything except, and I quote here, *"a unique and beautiful woman, born of Asian parents living and working in Canada and bringing the best of both worlds to her personal and public life.'*

'Would he understand you though?' Rosanna kept her tone light and even. She was getting breathless with eagerness.

'Oh yes he would!' she replied with an enigmatic little smile. There was a pause and Rosanna waited in vain for Tuyet to continue. Getting desperate and not liking the feeling one bit, she tried another question.

'How did Angus turn out to be your foster brother?....Tuyet?...' For a long while Tuyet stared ahead saying nothing.

'What?...I'm so sorry Rosanna. Our conversation brought back some wonderful memories and I got lost in time. What was your question?'

'Will I have any teeth left?' Rosanna wondered unlocking her jaw into a semblance of a smile. She could feel frustration mounting. It was becoming more difficult to maintain a congenial façade. 'Your foster brother, Tuyet?'

'You know my story I presume? The church assisted the families who had been on the boat with me but since my mother died during the escape, I was alone. Few people wanted to adopt a twelve year old without knowing something of my history.'

'It must have been a dreadful ordeal for you.' The remembered pain in her eyes was heartbreaking.

'Yes, it was but that is all past now. I was fortunate that the Howard family were willing to take me in, on the recommendation of the church pastor. Their love and kindness helped me through the worst of that first year. I lived with them for 12 years until I completed high school and college, learning the language and customs, trying to justify their faith in me.'

'Was it very difficult?'

'To be honest, yes and no. I was cut off from my former life and totally unable to articulate my needs, even after I could speak English fluently.

'What do you mean?'

'Most of the family discouraged me from talking about my experiences. They did so with the best of motives I'm sure. However, I needed to talk about what happened to me, to exorcize the horror, so to speak, and come to terms with it. Only Angus and Morag, who is so like him, understood. He encouraged me to read and to journal. He arranged for me to meet with other members of the Vietnamese community, to discuss the events that caused the conflict so as to come to terms with the struggle of my people. I needed to learn and accept that my parents did not die in vain.'

Rosanna could see that the hurt lingered. The dark eyes were filled with tears. She watched and waited for Tuyet to recover. The information about Angus explained why he knew about Tom Dooley and the work the naval doctor had done in Vietnam. Despite her breaking heart, Rosanna treasured the little things which connected her to Angus.

Huong, sensing a change in his cousin came over, most upset to find tears in her eyes.

'I know the cry' he explained in halting English. 'She think Vietnam. I tell her done now, but she still cry.'

'The loss of home and family is never done, Huong.'

'You Miss, you understand?'

'A little. It is better for her to cry than be angry.'

The cousins shared a few words in Vietnamese before Huong bowed himself away quietly.

'Please excuse me Rosanna. Huong means well, but his life is almost exclusively lived within a community that does everything much as they did back home. It is very difficult for him to know what I feel.'

'Don't forget I live in a bilingual world with my family too. Someday I'd like you to come home with me.' Rosanna had made the offer impulsively showing no regret when Tuyet beamed.

'I'd like that very much.'

'Are you feeling better?'

"I seldom cry anymore but you have been very …um… there's a word…sim…sim'

'Sympatico?'

'Yes, I like the sound of it. Did you know that Angus is…"

Her words were halted by a slight commotion at the door between incoming and outgoing diners. The sentence was never completed, much to Rosanna chagrin. They went on to talk about other topics, few of which satisfied her hunger for information about Angus.

At the restaurant door, a little later, the two women parted company amiably.

'It's been a very pleasurable evening Tuyet. I enjoyed both the food and the company.'

'Many thanks Rosanna. The pleasure was all mine. I hope I didn't burden you too much, with my stories.'

'Not at all.' demurred Rosanna squeezing the hand of her dinner companion. She knew the usual hugs and kisses which follow Italian goodbyes were not appropriate in many Asian cultures but habits die hard. She hoped Tuyet would not be offended.

It seemed not. The gentle pressure was returned and followed by a shy smile.

'We'll get together again soon.'

Rosanna remained deeply in thought after parting with Tuyet. She decided to walk the moderately short distance home. She hadn't really learned anything new about Angus. He seemed to be a great brother, obviously loving all his sisters. Cultural sensitivity was important to him both professionally and personally, but these were things she knew already. What she really wanted to hear, were stories about him growing up, what interested him as a student, how he made his way through college and medical school. She had formed a picture of him in her own mind but was desperate to flesh it out with details. The opportunity to explore each other's lives was lost to her during their brief, mostly emotional and physically charged weekend.

The anger she felt after their last encounter was gone. The initial fury had gotten her through the first few days but she was floundering again. Angus had been upset when he came to her. Their lovemaking was harsh, unrestrained and so very pleasurable, if she were honest. Still she had not touched the core of him, beyond knowing that he desired her.

She was more upset that she had not insisted on talking when he first saw her in the elevator. Their relationship was too new to withstand any deceit. It certainly couldn't be solved by a quick coupling. When Angus left he seemed so bitter. She didn't deserve his contempt but he had no way of knowing that. Thinking it may be better to just try and completely put him out of her mind she picked up her pace, vowing to forget Angus Howard, if her heart and body would also let him go. In spite of her resolve to avoid him, she was happy to have made a friend who would no doubt keep him in her orbit. Tuyet was good company and Rosanna hoped to share a meal with her again.

Chapter 13

Angus collapsed face down on his water bed. He was exhausted. Every long sinewy muscle in his body ached with fatigue and frustration. He had tried, without success, to banish the perfidy of Rosanna from his very soul but the warm brown-gold eyes and inviting smile continued to rise and haunt him through the depths of his anguish.

In an effort to combat the ghostly mist of her, he took to running again. In his early 20's when the taunts of his peers became too much for him to withstand, Angus had become the essence of the lonely, long distance runner. The care of his sisters had been misunderstood and despite his size, he continued to be teased unmercifully, first as a *mama's boy* then as a *queer*. He had no way of responding. Few understood the burdens sustained by his parents trying hard to stay financially afloat while caring for premature, partially handicapped twins. Ian's arrival only added to his mother's burdens. Angus and his father fought valiantly to keep their family from succumbing to the inevitable stress.

There was no time for extracurricular activities, sports, and dates. Angus, who considered himself rather pious had contemplated a career in the ministry until bitterness and anger forced him to realize that he couldn't overcome those feelings in order to be a good pastor. Pursuing medicine at university, as an alternative to theology, had also been a struggle, but very rewarding in terms of productivity. Marathon running had kept all other demons at bay and he was grateful for his success in both areas.

By age 35, with his life in order, a confident and secure man felt little need to continue the taxing requirements of keeping in shape. It meant sweeping changes and yet he weathered the inevitable let down, following his decision to stop competing. Changing his field of work from active pediatrics, to research had a lot to do with it.

The lottery win and Ian's subsequent revelations had only hardened his outer shell helping him to avoid further hurt and humiliation. Somehow those painful experiences did not touch the kindly inner core that would have made him an excellent pastor. Deep inside, he knew Rosanna cared for him. She didn't seem to be the type to play him for a fool. He thought he understood her values but could not understand her actions. All the discussion about his work was nothing more than a sham. That hurt more than anything.

Only a small part of the tortured man was dismayed by his conduct at her apartment. Despite his blinding anger, he would have desisted, if she had been adamant about not wanting sex. Rosanna welcomed him into her arms. He needed her desperately and could not resist her unspoken invitation. It was, as he said, mutually satisfying with no past or future to mar the performance, if that was how she wanted it. *But did she?*

He rolled onto his back, staring unseeingly out the window into the inky night. The pain in his throat and eyes, from unshed tears, still superseded that of his overextended muscles. *'I want to see her again and yet I dread it. Does she hate me or does she feel that I may be good for the occasional one night stand'?* Just thinking the words left him with a feeling of distaste. Angus knew that type of relationship raked against the moral grain of everything he valued. His hollow, mirthless laughter pounded mockingly in his ears. *'And yet, I'd take her on those terms!'* Angus directed his plea to the faceless easy chair which remained cold and unused since the day Rosanna left.

The looming impasse descended on him, blanketing his feelings. Where he once would have buried them and moved on, Angus felt unable to do so. In the quiet hours of the night his body ached for the fulfillment of a relationship too tenuous to sustain on his will alone.

Rosanna was fit to be tied. The committee meeting, with Angus present to defend his research plan and budget, was twelve hours away. Never in all her life did she have to battle nerves and fear as she did now. She had hoped that there would be some sign or word from him after he received the notification letter, but the phone was accusingly silent and junk occupied all the space in her mailbox.

'What is he thinking? Does he understand? Surely with his proven ability to forgive, he could see my name on the list of committee members and realize that my actions had been motivated by the demands of my job?'

Eventually a pounding headache forced her to take two

tablets and retire fairly early. A fatigued body, relaxed and sedated from the medication, enjoyed a peaceful night. Her mind and emotions did not. Rosanna would have preferred a miserable rainy day to match her mood as she prepared for work the next morning. It was, as expected in the sunny days of a July, a morning, clear and bright, mocking her somber thoughts.

Choosing an outfit suitable for the day suddenly became a major task, taking on epic proportions. She steadfastly refused to wear blue knowing how much Angus had loved her in that colour. She didn't want to make any covert statement to him. She chose instead a deep gold linen suit with a hip length double breasted jacket, to which she added black patent leather shoes and matching necklace and earrings. She might have looked a little overdone but she felt good and appeared attractive and professional.

The short ride to the hospital on the public transportation system failed to quell the butterflies which threatened to choke her. She schooled her features into a placid, pleasant looking façade hiding her inner turmoil. She was determined to present her strictly professional side, giving no one cause to question her.

Rosanna didn't know if she wanted the reprieve or not but by 9:15 a.m., her trembling hands needed to be hidden in her lap. She glanced at the ticking clock. There was still a forty-five minute wait until Angus would have to face the committee. The chairman was addressing her. She tried to give him her undivided attention.

'Ms Amadeo, I believe you were responsible for examining

the nature of Dr. Howard's research?' She nodded and he continued.

'Would you be so kind as to give us a brief outline of your findings for the benefit of those non medical members present?'

Rosanna had done her work well. She had been assigned to examine documents pertaining to her own previous field of practice. She could recite the detail ad lib, allowing her trembling hands to stay away from telltale paper rattling.

'Thank you Mr. Chairman. As you are aware, Dr. Howard's research has delved into the areas of foetal development which impact upon premature births, starting with the lungs…'

She spoke well, detailing the information, making it readily understandable by any lay person. Later she fielded questions and received kudos from her medical colleagues. Mr. Humphreys smiled and echoed everyone's praise. He paused before continuing, his voice deceptively patronizing.

'Thank you. That was very informative. We are not clear, however, in what way this information relates to the issue of budget keeping Ms. Amadeo.'

Rosanna wondered how this mean spirited man was chairing a committee so important to the hospital. She lowered her head and eyes, sensing a stirring around the table. Rather than raise her chin, ready to fight, as others might have done, she stayed quiet, head bowed. *'Even my father would not talk to me in that condescending tone. What a son of a …..'* Rosanna bit down on the last word. She was unsure if her tongue would find its outside voice.

'Mr. Humphreys, I don't think that we were required…..'

'It's fine Dr. Pappas. I am able to continue.'

Rosanna raised her eyes then, innocence written all over her face. A Mona Lisa smile, effectively hid her gritted teeth. Mr. Humphreys had tried to put her on the spot. Taking a discreet abdominal breath allowed a moment for Ms. Barclay's words to replay in her mind. *'This man is no dinosaur,'* she thought. *'He's a deceptively venomous snake.'* The change in metaphor from raging beast to ground crawler steadied her nerves and she spoke clearly and concisely to the group.

'As you know, grant recipients must prepare a budget to be included with their application taking into account staff, equipment, hours and stipends, but they must not step outside their stated goals. All other money contributed towards any project must be cleared in order to limit the possibility of bias in reporting findings and results.'

Rosanna droned on for an unnecessary amount of time. She had written proposals many times as part of her degree program and could recite the information off the top of her head. She shifted her papers once to give the impression of a prepared statement. Mr. Humphreys sat quietly. Using surprise, as a weapon of control and embarrassment, had backfired.

Rosanna concluded her information. The smile, by some supreme effort, remained sweetly in place. The meeting broke for refreshments but she steered clear, knowing her queasy stomach would repel even the lightest assault on its interior. Next on the agenda, was the interview with Angus.

∞

The charcoal gray lightweight suit fit him like a glove. He strode into the room apparently not in the least intimated by the members awaiting him. He showed neither remorse nor fear but exuded an air of quiet confidence. Angus avoided all eyes save those warm brown-gold long lashed beauties haunting him day and night. If Rosanna hoped for any sign of understanding, she was doomed to disappointment. The look she received was icy green and accusatory. It tore through her well constructed façade and pierced the essence of her being. *My God! He hates me. What have I done?'*

'Dr. Howard, thank you for coming in today.'

'I had little choice Mr. Humphreys. My career is at stake.' The words dripped from his mouth much like icicles falling from a winter roof into soft snow piercing the quiet landscape.

'A silent death,' Rosanna thought.

'Your words seem a bit excessive Dr. Howard. We are not here to question your professional skills, only the methods by which you work.'

'Same thing!'

'As you wish, Dr. Howard, but that is not our intention. This committee serves only to audit expeditiously in order that deserving causes such as yours may continue.' The words were said with just the right degree of rebuke, but the accompanying smile was only slightly warmer than a sneer. Angus said nothing more, but his stony gaunt face spoke volumes as he listened to Mr. Humphreys.

'If we could get on with the business here perhaps it would enable us to allow you to resume your work?' The chairman cleared his throat and continued. 'I believe you've met all of our members before?' Glancing around, he stopped then corrected himself.

'Perhaps you don't know Ms. Amadeo?'

'No Mr. Chairman. I don't know her at all.'

Rosanna stifled a gasp, fully aware of the double meaning behind the words. Tears threatened but were held in check.

'Yes….well she represents the nursing staff in the hospital.'

Angus did not acknowledge this information. The chairman was embarrassed. He plodded on with a mixture of disgust and smugness. His eyes beamed out a silent *'I told you so'* as if he could have predicted this kind of behaviour.

Rosanna was torn between humiliation and anger. Her Latin temperament and fierce pride stilled the trembling hands, raised the chin and enabled her to listen and participate in the proceedings. Angus remained barely civil keeping his further responses terse unless a longer explanation was absolutely required.

The chairman was clearly happy to end the session which had focused on the areas where the committee specifically needed to investigate. Expecting nothing more in the way of information he gave Angus an opportunity to speak.

'Do you have any questions Dr. Howard?'

There was a long pause. Angus seemed absorbed by the paper work on the desk in front of him. No one expected his next words. 'Is it your usual practice to try and garner information before the official proceedings?'

Mr. Humphreys bristled at the accusatory tone.

'It most certainly is not, Dr. Howard. I have no idea what you are talking about and I personally resent your tone and your implications.'

'And I, Mr. Chairman and members, resent your intrusion into my private life, but then I suppose ambition and politics often do make strange bedfellows.'

Rosanna knew her face drained of all blood. *'Is that what he thinks our weekend was?'* As cold as she had been minutes before, white heat and shame filled her with his statement.

All eyes were on Dr. Howard, questioning his words. The meeting suddenly threatened to get out of hand. The chairman stood. His red face had a strangely guilty look.

'Do you have any basis for your inflammatory comments?'

Angus glanced furtively at the blanched face of the woman he thought he might have loved forever. He couldn't be sure but whatever her motives were, it served no purpose to denounce her publicly or risk making his folly more fodder for wagging tongues.

'It's merely a question and a statement that I am entitled to make.' Angus replied with a nasty smile. His eyes were deep unfathomable aquamarine pools.

The Chairman did not like to be made to look foolish. He was not easily mollified. Temper led to indiscretion.

'Your conduct throughout this meeting has been as reprehensible as expected.' Humphreys paused taking a deeper breath than he seemed to need. Each member sat expectantly wondering what he would say next. The chairman's indiscretion was legendary.

'We have been far more patient with you than you deserve Dr. Howard. May I remind you that there have been reports of several people who benefited under questionable circumstances by the grant you received? If you hope to continue your work you would do well to remember that certain actions have consequences. This committee is also here to make sure that there has been no misuse of public funds before a federal inquiry is undertaken. Further unauthorized donations to any cause, however worthy, constitute fraud.'

Rosanna's horrified gasp was drowned out by the chorus of surprised voices. The slumping chairman fell heavily into his seat. A hidden agenda had been made public prematurely. The breach of confidential information was appalling but some would have agreed that the arrogant wimp in the hot seat should be silenced. He looked anything but contrite.

Angus seemed to listen to the chatter all around him. Nothing, except disdain, could be read in his stormy eyes. The meeting appeared to be drawing to a merciful and welcome end. Angus stood and surveyed his colleagues and adversaries around the table. Rosanna did not fall under his scrutiny. His gaze passed over her and she tensed waiting for him to speak. He began in the crisp voice she had not heard since their first encounter at the bed of the sick baby. His persona commanded silence.

'Gentlemen, let me educate you. Research is born out of a perception of need and a desire to find the answers which will fill the gap. Deceit of any kind invalidates both the result and the commitment of those who care enough to dedicate themselves to its service. The work must always be above reproach.'

Angus stopped. His commanding voice, with its powerful message, had been mesmerizing. The truth of his words rang out clearly. In those moments, listening to him defend his chosen role, Rosanna forgot their painful estrangement. She marveled at how principled he was even when under pressure.

Humphreys made a motion as if to stand but a look sent him back down into his seat. Apparently, Angus was not done.

'To defame my character, is to destroy the integrity of my work. Without my program, and the work of other researchers like me, the mandate of this committee becomes useless. Mr. Chairman, gentlemen, you would do well to remember that gossip and innuendo will not justify the existence of this group nor maintain its status in the future. My lawyer waits for my instructions. I bid you good day.'

With that final salvo, he exited the room, back stiff. There was no glance around the table to see the effects of his last words.

Mr. Humphreys had slumped in his seat. Dr. Pappas ran quickly to him checking his pulse and scanning him with a professional eye. Without the mantle of chairmanship he looked like a tired old man trying to unsuccessfully best a younger sharper tongue.

No one paid any heed to Rosanna. She quietly excused herself while the other members milled around waiting for the meeting to be officially adjourned. The Chairman seemed unable to continue and several others followed her lead. Rosanna's shaky legs and topsy-turvy insides made it to the nearest internal phone. She called her new friend.

'I can't explain now Tuyet, but today's meeting has been a complete disaster. I just don't feel well enough to do any more today.'

'Did Angus behave badly?' she asked picking up the tension in Rosanna's voice.

'We all did!'

'How can I help you? Is there anything you need?'

'Just let Ms. Barclay know I called and explain that I feel too ill to work the rest of the day. If she wants to see me in the morning, I'll make myself available.'

'Don't worry. I'll handle everything. Let me know if you don't feel well enough to come in tomorrow. Take care. Ok?'

'I will, thanks Tuyet.'

Rosanna rang off and made her way quickly to the nearest exit. She was hoping to reach home before her emotions could disintegrate and betray her . The sensations she was feeling threatened to overwhelm. Like a ticking time bomb, her spike heels clicked rapidly on the pavement. She neither heard nor saw anything. Each step was focused only on the need to get home.

The minute Rosanna opened her door she hated everything and anything in her way. A temper tantrum of epic proportions rose steadily, nearly sending her mad with the desire to destroy everything in sight. A horrible laugh welled up inside her. Tears and screams of rage alternated, bouncing off the walls of the lonely apartment. Hands clenched to stave off the oncoming onslaught of temporary insanity.

Rosanna made her way to the sun porch in the furthest corner of the living room. She hobbled on one foot, then the other, grabbing her shoes and flinging them in any direction. Uncaring of the path, the spiked-heeled missiles took off before falling harmlessly. The lazy boy chair beckoned. She tore off her outer clothes before sitting down, knees drawn up, shoulders hunched, her head bent in supplication. The curve of her spine was tense, the muscles knotted and pleading for release.

Trying hard not to lose control, she remembered the lessons of a much kinder time when she used meditation to help her cope with crisis after crisis, in a busy NICU. She ran through each muscle, forcibly pushing her blank, shocked mind to remember each group of tissue, willing the taut strings to relax one by one until her breathing was even and easy. Rosanna realized that this was no time for self pity. She needed to evaluate the situation objectively and try to make some sense of the heated words on both sides.

She knew now that Angus hated her. He had been disappointed in what he thought was a deliberate attempt to seduce him to further her own ambition. That hurt more than she cared to admit. It could also be resolved easily. Tuyet could confirm the date and time of her appointment.

Based on his belief, Angus had a chance to expose her but her didn't. *'I have to believe that he did it out of caring for me. It would serve no one if he were to denounce our weekend liaison'.*

Rosanna couldn't be sure but she surmised that self preservation was the likely motive. She didn't want to delude herself, but it was still very important to maintain a hope that he had a tenuous thread of feeling for her.

The most painful memory of the morning was not these things. When she spoke to Angus about his work, she had been so impressed by his commitment to succeeding, where others failed. He seemed to goad the incompetent Mr. Humphreys to make inflammatory statements and breech the confidentiality of the committee. The act of giving a voice to specific concerns was incomprehensible. '*Was it deliberate?*'

Rosanna and other sub-committee members were not privy to the same pieces of information as the members looking into the financial and accounting aspects of the audit. To say that Mr. Humphreys was out of line would be a major understatement. Those rumours and innuendos were unsubstantiated and therefore not for discussion. Their mission was a review, not a trial.

Since Angus knew the comments weren't true, she couldn't understand why he didn't say something, anything to show that everyone was wasting their time. Obviously the money used for personal benefit came from his lottery win. Rosanna jumped up from the chaise-lounge. Semi nude, she paced back and forth along the sun porch windows overlooking the main street below. Her thoughts ran into each other trying to sort through the emotions hoping to find the substance.

'*He doesn't seem to care. It is possible that what he considers my deceit is the final straw in a life filled with emotional abuse?*' Rosanna stopped pacing and leaned on the ledge, her forehead resting against the pane. Her hands were splayed out and pressed against the shatterproof glass as if she could push away the troubling events of the day.

'It's not true Angus. I do love you. Even if you hate me, don't give up on your work. It's too important. Surely it's worth fighting for.'

Impotent rage welled up inside her. She was tempted to resign the committee, if only to preserve her sanity, but it would be professional suicide. Rosanna understood there was no way she could help Angus, or depend on him to help her, if she didn't have access to the meetings. The fall-out from the proceedings would threaten everything. She was sure Angus intimated that he might end his research project, especially if he decided to seek legal counsel.

The clock was ticking towards 4:00 p.m. when Rosanna decided that she would take matters into her own hands. She made one quick call.

'Tuyet, I need to see you tonight.'

To say the woman on the other end of the line was surprised would be truly an understatement. It wasn't the request so much as the urgent manner in which it was voiced. After their talk over dinner, the bald statement was like a slap in the face. Puzzled by the change in demeanour and lack of warmth in the request, Tuyet hesitated.

'It's really important Tuyet. Don't ask any questions now. I'll explain when you get here.'

'Rosanna I…I..'

'Please, Tuyet….please?'

A sense of urgency and pleading, implicit in the words could not be ignored. 'Give me your address. I'll be right there.'

Chapter 14

Tuyet was shocked by Rosanna's appearance. The trip to the condominium was too short to speculate much about what happened. She knew that Rosanna had been ill earlier in the day, but she never expected the flushed almost frenetic nervousness which greeted her at the door.

The shiny black hair was untidy. The eyes were red-rimmed. They appeared to be bulging from the sockets. Rosanna wore a simple cotton frock. It looked as if she had slept in it. The hands, usually calm were constantly moving, wrapping and unwrapping themselves around her body.

'My God, Rosanna, what on earth has happened? You look......'

Tuyet trailed off not allowing her words to add insult to obvious injury.

'Don't worry, I know how I look. I am a mess! Since I came home at noon, I think every emotion I possess has been through the wringer.'

Tuyet tried hard to keep any distaste from her voice but she was clearly troubled. 'Are you sure you want to talk to me Rosanna? Don't you have family or someone closer to you who could help you better.'

'That's what you don't understand. I don't need someone to help me. I need someone closer to Angus. He's the one who needs help.'

'Angus?'

'Come on Tuyet,' she said, leading a somewhat bewildered and reluctant guest forward. 'Have a seat and please excuse the mess. My Latin temperament got the better of me. I can assure you it is not the usual me. I hope you believe that.'

Tuyet was more than a little uncomfortable. Rosanna knew that, like her relationship with Angus, she was expecting a lot of understanding from a short acquaintance. It took years to build friendships which could withstand personality changes and inappropriate behaviour. However, Tuyet had an all important binding tie with Angus. Rosanna was willing to do almost anything to help him.

She was certainly agitated but she did not forget her manners. Rosanna would not allow herself to be a poor hostess. The tea and cookies she had started to lay out after the telephone call were ready to be served. She cleared away any debris from the living room and set the tray in front of Tuyet before seating herself. She waited patiently for her guest to settle before speaking slowly.

'Tuyet….what I am about to tell you may shock or even anger you but don't judge me too harshly. I need your help and your discretion. I'm asking you to trust me.'

Tuyet, seated comfortably in a deep peach and rust patterned easy chair gave her full attention to Rosanna. She was able to suspend her judgment in the face of the unembellished plea. Her slight nod implied that she was also prepared to listen. Despite trying to remain calm, Rosanna realized that she had forgotten spoons for stirring the tea. She excused herself hoping that this further lapse would not weigh against her.

The reprieve gave Tuyet a few minutes to gather her thoughts as she listened to Rosanna rattle about in the kitchen. The self assured Vietnamese woman had faced many things in her relatively short life. More often than not she found her reading of people to be accurate. Tuyet didn't see Rosanna as an unworthy or easily intimidated person, nor was she blind to the faults of her foster brother. She was sure that whatever Rosanna had experienced, it could easily be resolved. Tuyet took a deep breath and whispered softly into her mind, '*I must be patient and objective. Rosanna will understand that Angus' happiness must come first*'.

∞

Over the plate of cookies filled with macadamia nuts and freshly brewed tea, Rosanna talked steadily. Occasionally she was interrupted by a comment or question from Tuyet. The story of the past month unfolded from the unadorned lips. From time to time, tears broke through, but the distressed woman spoke on sparing nothing, except details of the most intimate moments in the arms of her troubled lover.

'Rosanna, I can't believe that Mr. Humphreys could have been so unprofessional as to forget himself like that.' Tuyet spoke at last. Her voice dripped ice.

'You do understand Tuyet? I know you love Angus deeply,

but surely as Chairman, Mr. Humphreys' conduct was really inappropriate?' Her eyebrows drew together in a questioning frown.

'Of course! I've typed minutes from these meetings for years. I have never heard anything like it before. The committee is supposed to assess the work and review the budget. Why would Humphreys be pushing another agenda?' Tuyet threw out her hands. 'I know there's been silly rumors around the hospital. If Humphreys had proof that Angus had committed fraud, why didn't he report it to the hospital board? It's up to them to call in the police.'

'I don't get it either, but there seems to be more to it.'

'You're right Rosanna and I applaud your perception. He's a very insecure man. Over the years he's made remarks that I've often found offensive. I don't think he had much liking for Angus or what he perceives Angus to be.'

They were both silent for a moment each thinking about a fate they would like for the despised man.

'I really do love Angus. Somehow I have to find a way to help him.' The surprising admission broke the silence which had fallen.

Tuyet stared hard at the ravaged face knowing that her initial instincts about Rosanna had been correct. More heartening was the shared objective of putting her brother's happiness first. 'I can feel your love for him quite clearly. You have made the right assessment of his pain but I hope you realize that you must still respect your own position here, as I do mine.'

'I know Tuyet but I feel I can weather the storm of his lack of faith in me if I save his career. Somehow when I initially accepted the appointment I felt it would come down to this. His commitment to his research, I believe, exceeds what we had together and I want to preserve that if nothing else.'

'I don't believe you are making a correct choice Rosanna, but it seems to be the only one available at this time.'

'Even if we were to get back together, this whole mess will lay like a rock between us. No Tuyet, at all costs I must clear his name.'

'How can I help?' Tuyet was smiling, her eyes misted with unshed tears.

'Tell me about the lottery win. Everything is tied into the money. How long ago was it?' Rosanna's tone became brisk.

'Let's see….I remember that Angus shared in the very large jackpot not long after he applied for the grant. He didn't, for publicity reasons, come forward to claim his share. He had just been investigated and approved for the research grant. He wasn't willing to jeopardize the project.'

'Are they that strict?'

'I don't think so, but it was a chance he was unwilling to take. I believe he even contemplated using the money to get started but there were too many things he wanted to do for his own family. The internal struggle nearly did him in.'

Rosanna nodded, remembering his words about 'burnout' when he revealed Ian's revelations.

'How did he resolve it?'

'The grant came through about six months later. He secluded himself for three months planning and organizing the project then waited two months more before going for his own money. You have up to a year to collect. By that time, the nine days wonder of the big win was over. He was able to get his money with a minimum of fuss.'

'There has to be some way of proving it but short of photocopying a bank statement or the cheque itself, I don't know what to do.' Rosanna was chewing on a fingernail, her face intent with the effort of trying to solve the problem.

'I don't know if Angus would be willing to come forward, but then he would still have to prove or rather disprove the allegations before the final minutes are sent out to the hospital board of directors.'

'Do you think he would come forward?'

Both women looked at each other. Laughter bubbled up.

'It may be possible another way Rosanna. I think photographs are taken each time there's a winner, just for posterity or something.'

'But do you think they would have bothered, if he collected so many months later?'

'Yes, I'm pretty sure. Usually one of the conditions is that your name or photo may be used for publicity.'

'Where would I look?'

'Oh Rosanna, don't you buy tickets?'

'No I don't. Gambling is devil's work.'

Tuyet was shocked. 'But Rosanna, look how much good

the money has done. My cousin Huong is one of the many people who Angus was able to help. As for gambling, we all gamble at some time or another. What you are doing here carries more risk than buying a $1.00 ticket. The end result is not due to gambling. Angus is as stubborn as a mule and far too trusting. This is a dangerous combination. He has gambled his whole future, because he believes that truth will prevail. You will never get him to admit that sometimes, truth needs a helping hand.'

'I hope I can be that helping hand.' Rosanna was subdued, seeing the wisdom of her friend's words.

'We have a lot to do and secrecy is of the utmost importance. I intend to do a little digging myself. There's something very personal in Mr. Humphreys approach. I can't put my finger on it but he has a personal agenda. His attitude seems excessive for a routine audit. Let me know when you get the information Rosanna, and we'll figure out how best to present it to the committee.'

Both women were exhausted. The emotional ups and downs of the evening took a toll. It was clear to Rosanna that Tuyet was tired and getting ready to leave.

'Don't leave yet, please. I know it's getting late and I've been a terrible hostess. I could make a meal for us if you give me a few minutes.'

Tuyet looked pretty skeptical. 'I think I'd like to stay just to see what you can prepare in such a short time.'

Rosanna laughed. It was her first genuine release in days. 'The powder room is down the hall if you need it. Take your time.'

Tuyet soon discovered that Rosanna was right. The pair enjoyed a meal of veal lasagna, salad and garlic bread. They shared a small glass of red wine using it to toast the success of their venture.

Everything was homemade. The pasta dish seemed to melt in the mouth. 'How did you do this Rosanna?'

'To be honest, every time I go home for a weekend, my mother gives me dishes of home cooked food. Normally I freeze it so that there is always something to eat when I don't have time to cook. Salad doesn't take long and the wine is made by my father every year. I wouldn't be Italian if I didn't even have a mini wine cellar.'

'How little we know of each other.'

'But we are learning, and that's what counts.'

The evening had been interesting, revealing and tiring. Tuyet did not linger after dinner.

'I must go. Will you be in tomorrow?'

'Yes, I think business as usual is the best approach, but I may leave early, so I can do a bit of investigating.

At the door they affirmed the need for secrecy. The pair parted, satisfied that they could help the man who was so important in both their lives. Sleep came easy to Rosanna. She was emotionally and physically worn out. Few dreams haunted her night hours.

∞

Tuyet arrived home later than usual to the sound of a ringing phone. She immediately thought of Angus, wondering what she would say to him. He knew, as well as she, that they were not to be in touch. Wondering if he may have found it impossible to cope with the events of the day and needed someone understanding to share his feelings, she answered the phone quickly.

'Tuyet, where have you been? I have been calling you for ages.'

'I do have a social life you know, Morag.' Tension made her voice sharper than she intended.

'You are supposed to check with me, before you date any guys I haven't seen.'

'In that case, I'd never date anyone.' Tuyet replied without malice. She knew that her foster sister's personality allowed her to accept the disability and teasing without bitterness.

'You are too smart for me to cross verbal swords with you.'

Tuyet was disappointed. She loved the words games and challenges. There was no doubt that Angus was on her sister's mind. 'What's bothering you Morag. It's not like you to give up so easily?'

'I'm worried about Angus and you know why, don't you?'

'Oh yes, I know, but you also understand that I can't discuss it.'

'I know Tu, and I hate asking you, but he's so unhappy. Aunt Colleen hasn't been able to talk with him either.'

'Morag, please trust me. People who care about him are working very hard to help him.'

'Help him? I don't understand.' The older woman sounded genuinely puzzled.

'Then what are you talking about?' Tuyet queried, wondering what she had missed.

'Why, the woman of course!'

'The woman?'

'Yes, the woman! He's so depressed. I have never heard him talk with such sadness. Our dear brother is head over heels in love, but the woman doesn't care two pins about him. '

'That's not true!' The words were out before she could stop them. On her mind, was the risk Rosanna was about to take.

'Do you know her you sneaky one?'

'Yes, I do! Listen to me. If you repeat one word of what I've said, I'll deny it and I'll tell what's his name that you're cheating on him.'

''Ok, Ok I get it. No need to be mean. I won't say a word but, does she deserve our brother?'

'No Morag. She deserves more, but Angus is the man she wants. Now listen, try to keep up his spirits and pray that things will work out very soon. More than that, I can't say.'

'Can't or won't?'

'You taught me English so when I say can't, that's what I mean.'

'Ok, just reassure me once more.'

'Yes she does love him. How did you find out anyway?'

'I know my brother well. I've never heard him talk this way before. He's all tied up in knots, very irritable, little interest in his work. When I try to talk with him it is all about sighs and long silences. It's so unlike him. I am frightened.'

'Did you ask him directly?'

'Yes. He blew up and told me to mind my own business.'

'Not the first time he's said that.'

'No, but the tone of his voice was different. I could hear the hurt in it and feel the tension in his body when he hugged me to apologize.'

'He does have other problems Morag.'

'I know. He's always had problems. His whole life has been littered with stress, but somehow he manages to be kind and loving just the same.'

Tears came to Tuyet's eyes as she listened to the perceptive comments of the blind woman, who knew more about loving and giving, than many people who could see.

'Don't you start, Tuyet,' Morag chided hoping to stave off opening any of her sister's deep wounds.

'Can I ever do anything without you knowing?'

'No you can't! But, seriously, let me know if there's anything I can do.'

'I will. Remember, not a word, Ok?'

∞

Rosanna wasted no time. She was determined to begin researching the information needed. The lottery office was not that far from her residence or the hospital. Had she wished, the trip could easily be accomplished on a lunch hour. Choosing instead to start her day early then leave work before the lottery office closed, she donned a pair of comfortable low heeled shoes and braced herself for the unaccustomed exercise. To her delight, she wasn't as winded as she expected to be. With a smile on her face, she entered the glass encased lobby and was immediately excited by the photos which lined the walls. Surely Angus would be among the most prominent. He had received an outstanding win.

His unsmiling face did not immediately stand out. She had no doubt that embarrassment would have been his overriding emotion. No amount of success seemed to bring out the possibility of a fun loving man, thrilled by his achievements. One such human being, she knew, lurked below the surface of his solitary demeanour. Rosanna had seen that shadow self emerge briefly, during their short time together. Angus preferred hiding behind a wholly stoic façade.

As she made her way along the line of photos, Rosanna thought about how many times she had actually seen a warm unsolicited smile. She could recall just one moment. Her heart did little flip flops as she brought to mind the joy they shared at the makeshift breakfast table. Using pancakes to mop up the dripping syrup and butter from their plates, she had laughed at his persistence in feeding her. Angus responded with a look of unabashed delight. Her own pleasure was clearly reflected in his ever changing eyes. Her mind refused to move past visions of the early morning food sharing. Her body had already spent too much time reliving the intimate hours following their meal.

She had such high hopes for their relationship. Even in the light of day, Rosanna could not figure out how things could have gone so wrong. Ignoring the heart ache, in constant ebb and flow beneath the surface of her polite smile, she approached the receptionist.

'I wonder if you could help me. I am looking for a photo of a previous winner and I don't see it on the wall.'

'Do you have a date, Miss?'

'No, I believe it was approximately two to three years ago.'

'Are you kidding? We hold draws twice a week. If you don't have any idea of the date, you'll have to look through the book.'

'Would a name help?'

'No. We archive events by date.'

Rosanna sighed. She was directed to a small room upstairs. There were large books with photos of each winner. She picked two books within a possible two year time frame and sat down to search the photos. On her ninety second photo, an involuntary gasped escaped her lips. There was Angus, unsmiling as she had mentally predicted, accepting a cheque from the beaming lottery corporation director in the amount of four million dollars. Rosanna traced the face with her fingertips, lingering for awhile on the lean lines of his jaw. She longed to lean over and kiss the photo but stopped herself abruptly from behaving like love struck teenager, mooning over a movie star.

Disgusted with her silliness, she made her way back to the front desk and asked if the photo could be copied.

'Why?' asked the indifferent receptionist.

'Because I didn't get a copy of the photo the first time around.'

Apparently there was no satisfactory rejoinder. The young woman continued to look bored but she copied the photo reluctantly and charged a small fee, before turning her back to Rosanna, in dismissal. Happy with her success, she ignored the rudeness and clutching the photo as if it were a life preserver, she quickly exited the building. Along the way, Rosanna found a major copy centre, where a helpful young man made several larger copies, the date of the cheque clearly visible.

Happy with the small success of that trip, she returned home to type up a short note. It would accompany the photos.

Rosanna did not anticipate that much would change immediately. In spite of her doubts, she slept well for the second night in a row, the unsmiling visage of Angus clutched tenderly at her breast.

Chapter 15

One week later, the Audit Committee was in chaos. Mr. Humphreys had resigned in disgrace following the anonymous receipt of a letter and photographs confirming that Dr. Angus Howard had indeed received a considerable sum of money privately. The timing was a few short months after receiving the grant money.

Tuyet had also been busy. She discreetly befriended the former chairman's frustrated secretary. Some tidbits were revealed. It seemed that Mr. Humphreys' self-important daughter, was a paediatric specialist at another large hospital. It had been her failed seduction of Dr. Howard at a conference which sparked the personal infusion into the committee's activities. The father failed to believe that anyone could spurn his already once divorced, but highly eligible daughter. Humphreys concluded that the rumors about Dr. Howard were true and set out with no small amount of malice and cunning to destroy the man's career in an effort to salvage the pride of his only child.

Humphreys was responsible for much of the decision to

investigate Angus. He spent some time dropping several inappropriate hints around the hospital about Dr. Howard's character and financial affairs. A blind love for his daughter eventually cost him credibility and possibly his health. No one would know of his duplicity with regards to the motive but in light of the true facts, his behaviour at the last meeting was viewed with suspicion even allowing for Angus' conduct. As the committee members received the information with interest and concern, Mr. Humphreys lay quietly in bed, his foolish actions, and the embarrassing consequences, keeping his blood pressure at an alarmingly high level.

∞

Rosanna, like the rest of her colleagues was seated at the rectangle conference table, its rich oak finish polished to perfection. She stared hard at the photocopied picture and accompanying typed letter which explained Angus' new found wealth and the legitimate reason he had for spending so freely. It was her own proud creation, but no one would ever know.

Dr. Pappas had taken over for Humphreys as chair person. 'Members, I believe these papers are self explanatory. I don't know how they came to be sent to each one present here but I suspect that Dr. Howard was responsible for teaching us a lesson. Are there any comments?'

'Dr. Pappas, if I may?' The speaker was Mr. Gray, one the former chairman's closest allies. He proceeded when permission was granted. 'Does this mean, based on this letter and photo which I agree shows Dr. Howard to have been very fortunate, that this committee will discontinue the investigation?'

'Well, does any member, even with our limited knowledge so far, feel that a man who had just won over four million dollars would likely use a government grant to enhance his lifestyle knowing the risks?'

There were nods of dissent all around but Dr. Pappas continued wanting to be sure.

'Has any member so far found any indication that there was misuse of funds?'

Rosanna held her breath. There were nays all round again.

'Then members, I move that this investigation be dropped, a letter of apology be drafted to Dr. Howard. Then we can get on with our second case and try to put all of this behind us.'

The motion was seconded by Rosanna who could hardly contain her relief. She had been prepared to risk all of her professional status to repeat the facts surrounding Mr. Humphrey's misconduct if need be. Angus would never forgive her. Of that she was sure. This gamble had paid off. Angus would not be told the reason. Rosanna assumed that he would likely be ungrateful anyway. She did however sit proudly knowing that his work would continue. She was even able to delude herself into believing his research was all that mattered.

Later that evening, Rosanna sat on her porch and watched the sun setting. Its glorious colours should have made anyone glad to be alive. Rosanna remained quiet, sipping slowly from a glass of Papa's wine. Her earlier euphoria was forgotten. She had called her mother to share the news. Anna had not understood the deviousness that was necessary. She was, however, wholly satisfied by the simple answer to one question.

'Your man Rosa, he's free now?'

'Yes Mama.'

Anna knew that in time, if their love was meant to be, it would happen. Her often impatient child must learn that love like any precious thing needed to be nurtured before its full potential could be realized. She shared her thoughts with Rosanna.

'How can I nurture something that doesn't seem to exist?' She asked herself long after her mother's words were only a memory. *'To begin with, I need a nurturee. How silly I am'*, she thought, desperately longing for the warmth of the man, she very much wanted to see. Her thoughts were interrupted by the sound of the intercom.

'Oh my God! Angus!' Rosanna was rooted to the spot. The buzzer sounded again. She flew to the wall unit pressing the voice control with nervous fingers, hope reigning supreme in her heart.

'Rosanna, it's Tuyet. I've brought someone with me who wants to meet you. May we come up?'

'Yes, yes, of course.' It wasn't Angus, she concluded. He didn't need to meet her.

Surprisingly, the reprieve was overwhelming, informing her body that no matter how much she wanted Angus, the thought of reuniting with him scared her more. Heart pounding, she waited to see who was coming. She felt shaky but knew that it was important to get herself under control. In a moment of near panic, she wondered if she would always be so skittish. Her tired mind, waiting for the visitors to arrive, wondered idly what he was doing. '*Would he call or not? The messenger would have delivered the letter of exoneration already. Does he still hate me'?*

Rosanna was so caught up in her thoughts, she had forgotten in the space of seconds that Tuyet was coming up with a friend. It was too late to change her well worn jeans and faded cotton top. The knock at the door signaled the arrival of her guests. She wiped nervous palms down her thighs and opened the door.

It needed no second look to realize that the delicate fair-haired woman holding Tuyet's arm with one hand and gripping the tell-tale white cane in the other was one of Angus' twin sisters.

'Come in Tuyet and…..Morag.'

'How did you know it is not Meagan?'

She was a lovely woman, attractive, and unadorned. Her soft voice was high-pitched. She wore a simple blue dress which matched the near sightless eyes.

'Rosanna's very smart. Perception is not confined to you alone, you know. Come on, we are cluttering up the doorway.'

The trio moved forward into the apartment.

'Do you hear how she talks to me Rosanna?'

'I'm rather surprised. Usually she is so quiet and soft spoken.'

'Don't let that supposed genteel Asian façade fool you.' laughed Morag easily accepting the arm of her hostess. Rosanna guided her to a comfy chair. 'She is as outspoken as any one of us.'

'Ask me where I learned all about candor.'

Rosanna was amused by this sibling competition. The bond between the women was clearly a strong one.

'So how did you know it was me Rosanna?'

'Angus told me a little of his early life and I surmised that you would be the one most likely to come here. He told me that you were his best friend.'

'That's true, we were always out together. He takes pity on me.'

'Stop lying Morag. The way you dance, you make him look good.'

'My sister has no respect for me.' Morag's mock horror was comical.

'Rosanna called a halt to the banter. She offered refreshments to her unexpected guests.

Later, replete with iced lemon tea and homemade cake, the happy trio enjoyed a long discussion on the events of the past few weeks.

'Will you call Angus now?' Morag questioned. She was as blunt and direct as her brother had been when he asked for that first dinner date.

Rosanna hesitated. Morag waited, knowing by the deep sigh,

which followed her question, that the woman her brother loved, had also been deeply hurt by the misunderstanding.

'Everything between us happened so quickly Morag. There wasn't time to develop the kind of trust in me that would allow him to see beyond the obvious.'

'My dear, I can't see, but even in this short time I can feel that you love my brother. Tuyet told me you did, but she also knows I need to make my own decisions. That's why I am here, not to harass you.'

'That's the truth Rosanna.'

'I know. You are not harassing me. I appreciate that you took the time to visit. It only confirms every word Angus told me about his sisters. The thing is that I don't have to convince either of you. Much as I appreciate your support, only Angus matters. And...' she added with emphasis, 'I don't want either of you to speak to him for me. He must decide for himself whether I am his choice, warts and all.'

'Do you have warts, Rosanna?'

'Of course she doesn't Morag. She is quite beautiful. She is the pearl of a full moon on a dark night to the noonday sunshine of Angus.'

'My sister is very poetic isn't she? She has learned descriptive passages which allow me to 'see' in my limited way.'

Morag threw out a hand to Tuyet giving her a gentle squeeze of thanks. 'I have never been much for feeling faces unless I know someone really well. I prefer the vision of someone else, whose eyes I trust.'

Rosanna nodded, thanking her guest for her kindness.

Morag's blindness allowed the hostess to stare unabashedly at the face which was so very similar to the man she loved. A thought occurred to her, interrupting a mental foray into her memories of Angus.

'Morag, will you solve a mystery for me?'

'If I can.'

'Do you know who Annie is?'

'That's the name of the nurse who used to work with Aunt Colleen.'

'No…that's me!' Rosanna said through her teeth.

'I thought I told you that already.' Tuyet chimed in.

'Maybe you did. I forgot. Does she look like our Annie, Tuyet?'

The younger woman stared hard at Rosanna, her head cocked to one side. 'I don't know. Everyone looked the same to me in those days.' The two sisters laughed at the private joke while Rosanna seethed inwardly. '*What is so funny*'?

Refusing to ask any more questions, she sat glaring at the pair until Morag said, 'Rosanna, the story is not ours to tell you. My parents had many foster children over the years, Annie was one of them. Tuyet was, of course, with us the longest and would have been adopted by my parents if they had been younger, but social services would not allow it. Annie however was an unusual girl. If Angus doesn't tell you the story, then I will tell you on your wedding day.

Rosanna gasped. 'Aren't you being a little premature?'

'Yes, figuratively and literally but my early birth and

subsequent blindness doesn't stop me from seeing that you and my brother were meant to be together.'

'I'm sorry Morag.'

'Don't be. Your comment wasn't offensive to me, nor am I sensitive about myself. All three of us here have a common bond. The hand of fate has brought us together and I don't really think it was meant to be temporary. Now, I also think it is time to go. Tuyet?'

'Yes I'm here' she said extending her hand to clasp her sister's.

Rosanna had tears in her eyes. She wished she had the courage of Morag. The blind woman had a very knowing and loving heart. If things didn't work out, she hoped they could still be friends. Tuyet, and now Morag, had become very dear in so short a time.

'Keep in touch Rosanna. I live at home but I have my own phone. Call me if you want to talk.'

'I will Morag, and thanks.'

After they left, Rosanna went straight to bed. Not to sleep however. The words and feelings of the night washed over her. She was so grateful for the loving simplicity of her mother and the supportive warmth of Morag and Tuyet. As much as their kindness meant to her however, nothing could fill the void left by Angus.

∞

Friday was yet another long day. Each ring of the phone, each knock at the entrance of her cubbyhole office brought an attack of nerves followed by the inevitable let down when no word was forthcoming from Angus.

Tuyet called her on the internal phone after lunch. 'How are you feeling Rosanna?'

'I'm coping. There's been nothing yet.'

'Give him time. He does things slowly. Ms. Barclay wants to see you at 2:30. Is that convenient for you?'

'That's fine.'

Rosanna knew that Ms. Barclay would want to see her eventually. She had not given much thought to the possibility up until now, but the Director would want a firsthand account of the shocking events of the meeting. Five minutes before the appointment, she left her desk to walk the short distance to Ms Barclay's office. She stopped by Tuyet for a moment. 'I've asked my calls to come to you while I am tied up.' It wasn't unusual to forward calls, but the importance of the request was understood.

'Come in Rosanna. Have a seat,' the Director invited.

Rosanna had worn her lab coat over a simple gray dress which suited her mood of the day. She felt quite drab next to her superior's understated sky blue suit and crisp white blouse. As usual her face was benign and pleasant. There was no indication of her thoughts.

'Rosanna, I am sorry that your first experience, on a hospital committee was so….unpleasant. Your report was well written, however. I'd like to just add your personal thoughts to my own observations before I meet with senior management.'

'Ms. Barclay......' The pause was long. 'I feel I must be honest with you. The report contained only the facts but there are some things you should know.'

'Are you saying that there were pertinent facts omitted.'

'No. I'm not saying that. The facts are there. You asked me for my personal observations but I want to give you the full story.'

Ms. Barclay knew when someone was troubled. She closed the folder on her desk and removed her reading glasses. Rosanna received the director's undivided attention.

'When you offered me this job, I had just met Dr. Howard and we were developing a significant relationship'

The director frowned but said nothing.

'There was no contact once I understood where my responsibilities lay. It cost me his respect.'

'That could be easily remedied, I'm sure.'

'Perhaps, but I felt at the time that it was more important to clear his name because I was aware of his very genuine commitment to his work.'

'I don't think his commitment was ever questioned.'

'No it wasn't, but I underestimated his feeling for me. His perception of my actions created a situation in which he refused to defend or explain himself in the face of the accusations.'

'I have never known Angus Howard to back down. I admit I was surprised when these allegations were brought to my attention but I never expected the assessors or the committee to find anything significant. In my mind, the whole process was merely a formality and the stated financial concern would likely have its root in poor bookkeeping.'

'Yes, well the personal note introduced by Mr. Humphreys made it quite impossible. I was aware of the source of the financial discrepancy. I was also wholly responsible for the letter and the photographs attached to my report.'

'I see. You took a chance you know.'

'It was worth it.'

Ms. Barclay smiled holding out her hand. 'I will not reprimand you because I don't think your motives were self serving. I believe you have been true to your responsibilities. However, I do hope you will realize I can be your friend, as well as your employer.'

'Thank you Ms. Barclay.'

'There's no need for thanks. You have possibly saved Dr. Howard's career. You may, of course, continue your work with the committee. I hope that you will not allow a situation like this to get out of hand, without informing me beforehand. You report to me, not the committee chairman.'

'I understand.'

'I trust that you will be able to resolve things with Dr. Howard on a personal level.'

'Thank-you again'

Pleased that Ms. Barclay was as kind, in word and deed, as she appeared, Rosanna left the office giving Tuyet a discreet thumbs up. Tuyet responded with a smile of acknowledgment for the successful meeting but, a thumbs down on the unspoken question.

Rosanna returned to her office and worked steadily even though her mind was elsewhere. She was disconsolate. As soon as the clock was close to her finishing hour, she packed up and left. Once the audit had been completed she opted to work from an earlier morning hour. By four that afternoon she was headed out the door.

Her plan was to go home to Hamilton for the weekend. She was doubtful that he would call her and the anxiety was turning her inside out. She walked home in the warm July sunshine looking for all the world as if she had lost her best friend.

Angus was in a fever of impatience. The seminar was boring him to tears. All he could think about was the number of mistakes he made in his life. He wondered about the wisdom of making another. The less significant decision, to attend a function, in which his mind was not engaged, just added to his self abasement.

Moving his chair away from the table, he got up abruptly and left. His colleagues were surprised. They had been aware of the audit, but the hospital grapevine had been busy. Mr. Humphrey's indiscreet plan to destroy a respected co-worker closed their ranks strongly behind Angus. He couldn't have cared less about their belated support. If he had been tried and found wanting, they would have scattered pretty quickly, fearing the fall-out. Angus had no illusions about them.

If anything, he was unaware of how much his professional commitment was universally admired. As a researcher, his skills were rated as highly as any of the world's top Pediatricians. Angus never shirked his job or responsibilities. He wasn't, of course, required to attend the days' learning experience but leaving early was something he had never done before.

'He's probably still upset about the whole thing,' a sympathetic young Doctor offered.

'Well he's so arrogant, he's more likely upset because they wanted to audit him period!'

The argument ranged back and forth, in hushed whispers, behind Angus' fast disappearing back. The scandal and recent financial problems associated with his research project became far more interesting than the doddering old man mumbling ineffectually, at the lectern.

Angus meanwhile, sailed down the six flights of stairs of the south wing. He hailed a cab outside and went directly to his condominium. Anger, born out of frustration, churned within his gut. He could barely open the door of his home before he threw himself on the bed. The letter exonerating him lay in a crumpled ball between the pillows. It landed there after bouncing off a wall. When he threw it, Angus had hoped it would fall unheeded in some forgotten corner. Instead, the wrinkled mass settled comfortably in that spot, symbolically reminding him of the deep division this whole mess had created between him and Rosanna.

He smoothed out the tortured paper, reading again the words

that cleared him professionally. There was scant comfort. His thoughts always brought him back to the woman whose image haunted him day and night.

'Even if Rosanna believed in my innocence, even if she could forget the slurs on my character she will never forgive me for nearly exposing her to the committee.' Angus added disgust to his already overflowing cup of self blame. *'Surely her ambition would not stand in the way of a relationship. Maybe I could woo her slowly'.*

Angus was sure that despite her desire to gain an upper hand on the committee by accepting a date with him, she must have felt something. Their intimacy felt so genuine. *'I need her so much. Will she trust me again knowing that I, in my anger hurt her so badly?'*

Angus returned to the easy chair, the first time since Rosanna left his condominium over a month ago. He sank into it slowly holding the memories at bay.

'Suppose I was wrong about her? Suppose she was innocent, really felt something for me?' His hollow laugh echoed around the room. If real feelings were involved, he conceded that she would have every right to hate him, for having so little faith in her. Either way, he considered that she was lost to him. Angus knew loneliness so deep and so profound he was unable to breathe with its intensity.

The days ahead stretched bleak and empty. In his mind's eye he saw the vision of a midnight highway stretched across an arid desert. *'My past is lost in time, my youth gone, my future beckons only as a gray mist.'* The switch from melancholic self pity to poetic thoughts intrigued him. Angus had never been one to be absorbed by the mysteries of life. His love for Rosanna opened quixotic doors in his mind. Logic, reasoning and caution had no place when his heart ruled his head. Angus realized that for the first time in his life, he had to act on his feelings.

The decision made, he jumped up from his chair. His long finger traced the spines of several books along one library shelf. He was searching for a particular but seldom used book. A similar volume stood out in the midst of the books in Rosanna's library. Even though he knew so little about her, he was certain that none of her books sat on the shelf without being read. Remembered snatches of their conversation affirmed that he was on the right track. Angus opted to use a traditional version to declare his heart's outpouring, hoping that the wording would generate curiosity and draw her attention into the meaning.

Once located, he removed the long sleeved shirt he had worn to the seminar, flexed his shoulder and hand muscles before settling again in the chair. The physical preparation was as necessary to him as the intense warm up for a long run. He searched page after page intent on finding just the right passage which would express what he was feeling. It took some time but copying the expressive sonnet gave him no small measure of satisfaction.

A plain white envelope was found and the words of his heart were carefully sealed inside. The name of the object of his campaign was scrawled impatiently on the smooth white exterior. There was no hesitation now. He had risked a small bet on a whim and won. Today he was risking everything, hopeful that the words of a long dead poet could save a love as timeless as the words themselves.

Chapter 16

Rosanna had certainly made up her mind to go to Hamilton. Somehow she continued to procrastinate finding numerous unimportant chores to keep her from leaving town. It was nearly 5:30 before she pulled up short, realizing the futility of prolonging the inevitable. *'I'm leaving! I'll just take a shower and wash my hair first,'* she thought trying to console herself with a final totally unnecessary action. So it was that Rosanna was lost under the sounds of flowing water and fragrant shampoo bubbles when the intercom demanded her presence at the door.

Angus, in the lobby and praying for a quick response to the insistent ringing, was dismayed at being thwarted in his efforts to resolve issues. He reluctantly left his plea in the hands of the security guard in the foyer. Strict instructions, to see that Miss Amadeo received it as soon as possible, were strongly emphasized.

The disinterested young man nodded carelessly and placed the envelope at the edge of the desk. A burning glare from Angus changed the attitude in a hurry. The white square soon sat directly under the nose of the guard where it would not be forgotten.

'Please try again in about an hour.'

Angus would have waited intent on ensuring that his instructions were carried out but he was deeply disappointed and unsure what to do next.

Rosanna, unaware of the scenario playing out in lobby, ended her long and delaying shower with a thumping heart and endless sighs. *'Cleanliness is next to Godliness,'* she chanted drying her hair in the mirror and hoping to fill her mind with nonsense. The powerful sound of the hair dryer effectively blocked out a knock at the door of her condo. Unaware of any urgency, she continued to style the thick dark strands, wondering why she was bothering. Rosanna really had no desire to go home. She wanted to stay in her own home. *'No, I want to go to Angus' home,'* she decided getting to the heart of the matter. *'I want him to tell me that he doesn't care. I want to hear it from his lips.'*

A thought struck and she allowed her honest desires to bubble up to the surface of her consciousness. *'Why don't I just write to him explaining what happened? If he reads it directly from me, perhaps he will feel differently, see things my way'.* Rosanna knew she was getting into her endless back and forth internal arguments. She didn't want to trap herself in the useless circular mental processing. Action was called for. She gave some thought as to how she would mount a campaign to win him over. Nerves failed her at every new idea, but she forged on, knowing that to take no action would have the least desired result.

Of one thing Rosanna was certain. Angus was as much of a reader as she was. In her brief time at his apartment, she had found a moment to survey his collection. Only the books which she herself had read, stood out from others, but she knew that he came from a background filled with literature. Rosanna had no shortage of language skills but somewhere in the vast world of words, the meaning had to be unique and yet readily understood. She chose her inspiration carefully feeling the need to try something familiar yet different.

The hair was perfection when she put down the dryer on the bathroom counter and headed towards her small library of books. She knew the exact location of what she was looking for. After a moment of thought, she pulled it towards her. The edges were well worn. Unerringly, she found the sonnets written long ago by a man of extraordinary vision. His poetic words covered every human emotion known to mankind. She seated herself at the small desk located on the sun porch. Her hands were soon busy writing, copying, word for word, the exact thoughts and feelings she wanted to convey.

Before a lack of courage could defeat the plan, she hastily sealed the short note in a pale mauve envelope. Rosanna grabbed her purse and headed directly for the underground parking. Calm settled on her. Rather than trying to imagine the outcome, she followed her heart and prayed instead, that he would understand the meaning.

Like Angus, her mission was doomed to disappointment. She reluctantly left her tender communiqué in the hands of a well dressed, security guard whose elevated eyebrow made her think twice about the very casual attire she'd worn. Rosanna knew that some very important people lived in the condominium complex. The guard clearly had to be on the lookout for undesirable and unscrupulous types. He treated Rosanna like a groupie. The guard's disdainful look said as much. Since Dr. Howard was not the famous rock star who lived there, the man agreed to deliver the envelope.

Neither Angus nor Rosanna reached home before 10 p.m. They couldn't face their lonely apartments. Each had wandered aimlessly around the city on the hot humid summer night. Faces, people and activities were all a blur. Loneliness cocooned them in separate worlds of their own. There was lots of time for introspection but it all came to naught since the half needed to make the whole of their existence remained elusive.

Angus received his note first. He didn't immediately recognize Rosanna's handwriting. By process of elimination, he excluded almost anyone else's. This was a new. The supercilious guard at his door was inclined to linger and explain his reason for accepting the note. Unimpressed with the whys, Angus grabbed the letter and pumped the shocked man's hand. He was already tearing open the envelope, well before reaching his apartment door. Never, for one moment, did he anticipate bad news but the unusual contents caused a frown. He had to read it several times before it made sense to his anxiety plagued mind.

> Dear Angus, it read

> Accuse me thus: that I have scanted all,
> Wherein I should your great deserts repay,
> Forgot upon your dearest love to call,
> Whereto all bonds do tie me day by day;

'Rosanna you didn't exactly give me the chance to really show you what an honest love could be like. Everything you did, told me that you didn't care. What was I to think?' Angus was

deeply puzzled, wondering what he had said which could have turned her away. Only the idea that she had used him to further her career, made sense to his anxiety plagued mind.

> That I have frequent been with unknown minds,
> And given to time your own dear-purchas'd right;
> That I have hoisted sail to all the winds
> Which should transport me farthest from your sight.

'Is that why you disappeared? Did they make you think of me as a bad person?' Angus was restless, wondering if she had separated herself from him for other reasons. He read on…

> Book both my wilfulness and errors down,
> And on just proof surmise, accumulate;
> Bring me within the level of your frown,
> But shoot not at me in your waken'd hate;
> Since my appeal says I did strive to prove
> The constancy and virtue of your love..

'She thinks I despise her. How could she feel otherwise? My love? My love?' Angus' mind pondered the question, seeking answers from within. It was difficult but he was beginning to realize that perhaps it wasn't his love of her which she needed to protect, but the love of his work. He kept his thoughts closed to his own, most recent actions knowing that they clouded his judgment. Free of the mental blocks which ruled his emotions, Angus experienced a physical wave of emotion during which everything became almost clear. It was the same sensation which came to him the moment he looked into Rosanna's eyes in the bookstore.

∞

Rosanna returned to her parked car. For hours she had walked the Queens Quay-Harbor Front area trying to determine exactly how she felt. Despondency was painting a very grim picture of her future. It was impossible to face another day with this uncertainty. The courage which lay at the heart of her letter writing deserted her. She sat for some time, enclosed in her car, leaning her head back breathing deeply. Images of Angus floated through her mind. Every time Rosanna felt that she could put him out of her life, she would suddenly feel a surging, urgent need for his touch. She closed her eyes remembering the short, bittersweet time she was last in his arms.

For a few moments she was lost in waves of delight. *'Oh my God!,'* she shouted into the unfeeling steering wheel. The delight she expected to feel turned to horror. Rosanna gripped the round object fiercely fighting the desire to bang her head against it in pure frustration. *'Not again! How could I have been so stupid?'*

Just like an ugly monster which plagues nervous dreams, Rosanna knew something had been pushed to the back of her mind for the past weeks. The last time she and Angus had been together, they didn't use any contraceptive. It was the right time of the month and she was ten days late already. Her biological clock had been forgotten in the stress of the last few weeks.

One thing she knew was that she could not ask Angus to come to her now. She believed based on her past experience, that he would think she wanted to trap him. *'I should never have left that note. What am I going to do?'* She turned on the engine with shaking fingers and made her way home slowly, seeing her life fall to pieces before her eyes.

She parked in the underground of her building but exited at the street entrance to head to a nearby all night pharmacy. She had seen the ads for home pregnancy testing and knew that it wasn't too soon to check.

Returning home a short time later, the white bag clutched in nervous fingers she was stopped by Alex, the regular night guard.

'Hi, Ms. Amadeo. Are you alright? You seem kinda pale.'

'No….I'm…fine…. thanks. It's ok Alex.'

'Ok Miss. There's a letter here for you. I hope it's not bad news. Randy said some guy left it here this afternoon.'

'This afternoon?'

'Randy said you were out when he came. He told me that the guy seemed worried and wanted you to get the letter right away.'

Rosanna tilted her head and raised her eyebrows in a silent query.

'Randy didn't know who you were and couldn't find you. Here it is Miss.'

Rosanna stared at the envelope. An unreadable look appeared to increase the tension in her face. She had been home earlier, but said nothing knowing it would create discord between the guards.

'Are you sure you're alright Miss? Do you want me to wait while you open it?'

Concern was written all over his face. Rosanna knew he took a special interest in her. He was always on duty when she left for work at night. They had spent many months sharing a few words. He hadn't seen her for a few weeks and wondered if she had been ill.

Rosanna was rooted to the spot. Alex had every right to think she was sick.

'No really Alex. I'm fine. Did you say it was left this afternoon?'

'Around 4:30-5:00.'

'Are you sure?'

'Yes Miss, we keep a record of things like that.' It wasn't true but he wanted to sound important, sensing that the timing was valuable to her.

'Well thanks. I'll just go up, I think. I'll be fine.'

'If you are sure Miss. Call me if you need anything Ok?'

Rosanna refused to open the note until she was safely inside her door. She was sure that Angus was the one who left the letter for her. She wanted more than anything to believe that he still wanted her but the uncertain part of her psyche felt that he intended to put the final nail in the coffin of their romance. The key to her future lay in the white bag in one hand, or the white envelope in the other. She did not think that the two could be reconciled.

Seated in the privacy of her bedroom she looked at the bag first then the letter, hesitating. In the end the decision was removed from her hands. The elusive specimen wasn't forth coming so she sat yoga style on the bed and opened the envelope.

It read,

Dearest Rosanna,

> *Your love and pity doth th' impression fill*
> *Which vulgar scandal stamped upon my brow;*
> *For what care I who calls me well or ill,*
> *So you o'er green my bad, my good allow?*
> *You are my all the world, and I must strive*
> *To know my shames and praises from your tongue;*

'Oh Angus, I can't find one thing which is bad about you. In so short a time you became the world to me as well.' she thought fingering the paper lovingly and tracing the words as if by doing so, her weary heart could read and be comforted by its message. Rosanna retrieved the picture of her heart's desire, continuing to read between the lines of his apology. She wished with everything in her and from the depths of her soul to be able to tell him exactly the words of praise which he needed to hear.

> *None else to me, nor I to none alive,*
> *That my steeled sense or changes right or wrong.*
> *In so profound abysm I throw all care*
> *Of others' voices, that my adder's sense*
> *To critic and to flatt'rer stopped are.*

'You crazy fool! Do you really believe that you can ignore the world and neglect your work because of me?' The tears which fell were strictly a release. Her admiration for his research knew no bounds.

> *Mark how with my neglect I do dispense:*
> *You are so strongly in my purpose bred*
> *That all the world besides methinks y'are dead.*

'Oh Angus,' she laughed and cried, simultaneously throwing

herself back and hugging her pillow. '*How on earth could you believe that I would give credence to those accusations against you or that they could change my mind about you or us?*' His lack of faith in her was only mildly disturbing. They hadn't the time to develop a trusting relationship. Angus previously had been hurt by people who obviously claimed to love him. It would have been very difficult, in the best of circumstances, for their new love to survive the ups and downs of the past weeks.

Rosanna knew she could convince Angus that she cared. '*I've got to call him now.*' She reached over to grab the phone on the night stand, only to realize that she didn't have his number. Sinking back in the hopelessness of trying to find his number at such a late hour, she was startled by the buzzer.

Oh please, please, don't let me be disappointed, she prayed silently, running to the small foyer. *If it's Alex checking up on me, I'll scream.*

'Miss Amadeo, it's me Alex.'

'Yes Alex?' Rosanna gritted her teeth thinking again about the need to call her dentist to check if she had any enamel left.

'Are you Ok?'

'I'm fine!' The words were emphatic and abrupt. She had enough.

'I'm sorry Miss, but the man who says he dropped off the envelope is….'

'Send him up!'

'She says it's ok sir.'

'Please hurry Angus, please,' Rosanna mouthed in a fever of impatience and joy. She stood by the door, hand on the knob, ready to open it at the first knock. She stood on tip toes, feeling her body absorb an amazing energy. *'What am I doing? Forget this!'* she told herself. Turning the handle, she released the last barrier to their love and ran down the hall, hopping back and forth as the muffled whirl of the elevator came closer and closer.

At last, the doors parted! Angus stood before her, uncertain, his face so dear. Rosanna held out her arms and he swooped her up with an ecstatic moan, carrying her wordlessly to the condominium. Inside, the door was slammed with a resounding thud as the pair hugged and kissed and kissed each other endlessly. Rosanna held his face murmuring words of love and comfort to the man whose arms supported her tightly. She was his lifeline to sanity.

'Angus, Angus, I love you so much. I never wanted to hurt you. I never believed those things about you. How could you think that?' Her words were punctuated by kisses to every part of his face and neck not covered by clothes.

Angus was so overwhelmed by her reception. It was more than he expected or hoped for. '*So are you to my thoughts as food to life,* my love, but I need to talk with you, please my darling.

'No! no more words Angus. Just kiss me, please.'

Angus obliged, wanting nothing more from life than to please this woman for the rest of his life. Reality surfaced. He hadn't moved from the foyer and his arms were getting tired. Reluctantly he let her go and they made their way to the couch. Memories of their last encounter there simmered below the surface but did not intrude in a negative way. They sat curled up, side by side, knowing that they had to clear up the understandings. Angus hushed her with a finger.

'Rosanna, I know I've behaved badly. I've been hurt so many times. I think I allowed my past to cloud my judgment. I said words and did things which made no sense to me, but it was even more painful to see the hurt I caused you.' He paused, breathing deeply, holding her eyes to his with a power he was just beginning to release, before she spoke again.

'Please stop Angus. I don't want you to blame yourself. I accept my share too. We had such a wonderful weekend but hardly enough time to get to know each other properly. It was right after our time together that I found out about my appointment to the committee.'

'What? Oh my God! I have been so foolish. I thought you used me to further your career.'

'Angus please, I told you the blame is mine too. I should have told you about it or at least that I was to be a part of it, instead of running away, but Ms. Barclay put so much emphasis on avoiding you. She changed my shift so that I would avoid even Colleen for that matter. I was so terrified for the safety of your work that I...'

'You stayed away to protect me?'

'Well yes...Ms Barclay said...'

'I don't care what she said. What you are saying? ...Rosanna could you love me that much?'

'But Angus….I told you I love you. Didn't I? Your work…. it was so…. important to you.'

Angus was unable to articulate a word in defence of his thoughtless actions. His sorry countenance hurt her heart.

"Love is not love, which alters when its alteration finds" she quoted the great Bard in a gentle voice, hoping to take away the look on his face. 'I love you.'

'Rosanna' he breathed out on a releasing whisper and holding her face in his hands. 'Can you ever forgive me? If it takes the rest of my life….'

'I don't want those promises Angus. You came back to me still believing the truth of my deceit. Your love has been as constant as mine and we have weathered this storm. Let's not dwell too much on the past weeks. I only want to look at what's ahead.'

He kissed her then, threading his fingers through the thick silky black hair, stopping once to gaze deeply into the warm gold brown eyes. The tip of his tongue strayed to her lips delighted when they parted inviting him in. It wasn't long before the kisses were not enough. He found the softness of her flesh, as his hand slipped beneath her clothes to massage her tenderly.

'Angus, let's go inside.'

They made their way to the bedroom, totally feminine in its frilly white and pale blue colours. Angus followed Rosanna into the room, his hands on her shoulders. There, in the middle of the rumpled bed, lay the tell-tale pregnancy testing kit. They were brought up short. Rosanna had forgotten about it and she was embarrassed. Angus questioned its existence with a noticeable frown.

'I'm sorry Angus, I didn't mean for you to see that now. I…I…I'm late and I just wanted to make sure after our last…when you were here…you….well you didn't….'

'Rosanna, it could be stress you know.'

'Stress? I suppose it could be. I never used it though. I couldn't……well, you know .'

'There's no need.'

'No need?'

'No my sweet love, I was very angry that night. I wanted to love you and hate you at the same time. My words were unkind but I've seen too many innocent children suffer to take a chance on bringing one into the world without stable, loving parents, raising them as a unit.'

'You mean you didn't….?'

'No I didn't release myself. If I did, I would never have been able to leave. I thought you realized that. I know I wanted you to hurt as much as I hurt but as I looked at you, I realized that I didn't really want to be responsible for causing any sadness in your face or your heart. And yet, I did.'

Rosanna knew a profound relief that he didn't even question the existence of another man. His arms encircled her wanting to offer a final reassurance.

'You should know how a woman's body will often react to stress. Your normal cycle was thrown off course and….'

'You sound like my doctor, doctor.'

'Not a bad idea Rosanna. You obviously need a thorough check up.'

'I don't need that kind of doctor' she murmured huskily checking his face, partially shadowed in the soft lamplight.

'No, I believe you are right. I am after all a pediatrician. I would rather be the doctor of our children.'

'Is that a proposal?' she gasped.

'No, it is a statement of fact' he declared rubbing her back lightly.

'A woman likes to be asked you know.' She pushed at him to emphasize her point, but was too happy in his arms to be dismayed by his un-lover like attitude.

'Your body has already sent a message I can't ignore, however…..' he paused releasing her to get down on one knee. Taking her left hand he kissed it warmly.'

'Angus, get up. You're making me laugh and this is a very serious matter.'

He stood up quickly. The naughty boy look was back on his face, before it changed to one of seriousness. Taking both her hands in his he said

'Rosanna, I am a scientist. I have never been good with loving words but it's difficult to ignore your feminine, romantic appeal. That is the side of you which has tempted and haunted me these last weeks. Your warm and giving nature stirs so much of the good that's left in me, that I can believe I'll feel whole again. I want to be with you, love you, hold you in my arms until nothing matters except what lies between us. I want it to happen with you as my wife. I love you so very much. Will you have me?'

Rosanna gasped again, with stunned surprise. Feelings she never knew, surfaced making words impossible. She nodded her assent, too full with emotion to say the words.

Angus held her lightly searching her moistened eyes intently for any doubts. There were none.

At last, when she could speak, Rosanna held the face of her dear beloved, whispering softly.

'I love you Angus. In all my life, I have never felt so complete as I do in this moment. I feel that your soul and mine belong together, have always been together.' Nodding her assent she answered his question. 'I will have you as my husband.'

They kissed tenderly to seal their commitment to each other.

It wasn't long before the kisses deepened, asking and seeking more from the loving couple. Their tongues met straining to satisfy the yearning their bodies had held in check. Angus reluctantly left the moist lips, planting tender kisses on her eyes then onward to her ears, breathing softly in the pink hollows before caressing the line of her neck.

The trembling body held securely in his arms became agitated as need devoured her.

'Rosanna, help me please my love?'

She did as he bid, unbuttoning his shirt with eager haste, holding his eyes as the shirt fell away. Likewise, her simple top was pulled off. The bra quickly followed. Their mouths met again while buttons and zippers were undone until naked at last, they held each other, hands kneading the taut flesh.

The unused box fell unheeded to the floor as they tumbled on to the soft duvet, arms and legs entwined, rolling back and forth, rocking with a steady rhythm as they sought fulfillment.

Rosanna lost all sense of time, feeling only the aching pulsating desire for Angus to fill her. She cried out as his mouth found the hardened peaks of her breast. He kissed each one tenderly while his fingers found the soft flesh of her sexual being. She gasped as wave after wave of delight sent fiery sparks through her body.

'Angus...Angus...please...'

Never in his entire life did the man loving the deliciously tortured woman on the bed feel so close to another human being. He wanted to worship her body. Stopping his ministrations to look at her face he was halted by the expression of frank sexual need expressed there. In the past he might have shied away from responding wholeheartedly, but he knew he was wholly responsible for the desire and love beckoning him. It struck a responsive chord in a body long held in check. Rising above Rosanna he continued to hold her eyes with his own. He paused in the observations of her loveliness.

'I wish to capture this moment forever Rosanna. It is as if something magical has happened and we are suspended in time. This memory will always be nearest to my heart. I'll never hurt you again my love.'

As he entered her deeply, she cried out his name. The sound was wrenched from the depths of her very soul. Rosanna wrapped her arms and legs tightly around his glistening body. She drew the blond head to her lips drawing the very breath from him as she strained upwards to meet the powerful strokes.

'Just love me Angus…nothing more…just love me as I love you.'

'I do my love…I do.'

Words were impossible then as Rosanna felt her body float free, rising, reaching the incredible high only love can bring. She felt Angus pull away as his own climax shook the muscular frame. She held him to her. A barely perceptible look in his eyes questioned her, but she held him tighter as feelings rose again inside her.

This time they floated together, their bodies rocked and twisting with the sweetest joy.

Chapter 17

Hours later when the happy couple resurfaced, Rosanna could not make sense of the events of the night. She never imagined a love or lover like the man who lay by her side.

'Angus, I am so disoriented' she admitted with a sigh. He opened a sleepy eye.

'My darling, you are in my arms where you belong. I have never been in this room before, but where ever you are, I know I am grounded.'

Had they not been so tired, the words might have generated more of the intense love making, but they were satiated. Rosanna realized they had fallen asleep in an awkward position and attempted to right their twisted bodies. They settled beneath the covers, not ready for more intimacy, but needing to talk and share a little more of their incredible feelings.

Angus was still inclined to self blame. 'I have been such a fool' he sighed into her neck.

'No recriminations, please? There will be enough facing us in the future.'

'What do you mean? The business at the hospital is behind us. I know my family will love you.'

Rosanna smiled in response to this. Angus could feel the movement of her lips against his skin.

'What's that smile for? Don't tell me they have been bugging you already?'

'Well, Tuyet helped me quite a lot. Without her, I doubt that I could have found the courage to continue. After the committee cleared you, Morag paid a surprise visit to check me over and make sure I was right for you.'

'The little minx! How could she?'

'She loves you Angus and she believed I had hurt you.'

'And Tuyet..?'

'I don't want to get into all the details now but she supported me after that disastrous meeting, encouraging me to do what I had to do, to make things right. She said I should have faith in your common sense. You know, she was right!'

'I wish she could have been my sister by law. In those days, Morag was so restless, wanting something to do at home. As twins, the girls had always been close but when Sam showed an interest in pursuing a relationship with Meagan, Morag felt left out. It wasn't intentional, but when my parents started taking foster children, Morag became their surrogate mother. Tuyet was a delightful girl giving as much as she received. She kept Morag company and helped her fill time while I was away studying.'

'They are very close Angus and I'll enjoy having them as my sisters-in law but they are not the problem. I was thinking about my own family. My parents are very Italian and they won't take kindly to me marrying a man who can't communicate with them and one who is not a Catholic. They will respect your religious beliefs but it could mean bumpy days ahead.'

'And your brothers and sisters?'

'Luke, Terry, and Pat are ok but….'

'Luke, Terry and Pat?'

'Ok well, Luciano, Theresa and Pasquale,' she laughed realizing that the non-Italian names sounded very odd from old fashioned Italian parents.

'They are the youngest of my siblings. Luke's wife is Irish, and Terry's husband is Italo-Canadian. Pat's not married but Domenic, the eldest, will stand squarely behind Papa when they look you over.'

'Rosanna, I am not worried. You love me and I love you. All parents only want to see their children happy. Whatever the obstacles, we will overcome them. I want to ask your father for your hand in marriage….and as soon as possible. I certainly don't want you to be walking down the aisle five months pregnant!'

'I'm sure it will be alright this time, but we won't take any more chances after tonight.'

'No' Angus murmured seeking her full lips again. 'Just for tonight it will be alright.'

∞

The following Sunday Rosanna and Angus drove to Hamilton to meet her family. She had yet to meet his parents but they agreed to postpone the get together until after the all important question to Rosanna's father. She was worried, and tried to hide her concern from Angus. In his arms, she knew without a doubt that he was the only one for her. In her quiet moments alone she did fret about the reception he would receive at home. They would be married regardless of what her family thought, but it would mean so much more to have the unqualified blessing of her parents.

The Sunday morning, in late August, dawned bright and clear. The roads were deserted. The last summer weekend sent people scurrying out of town. The golden blond and midnight brunette heads moved very little as the pair in the car headed west. They were each busy contemplating the scenario ahead, but they held hands between the bucket seats.

Angus drove the powerful Jaguar at a sedate pace along the highway. He knew Rosanna had tried to hide her concern. He wanted to reassure her, but experience taught him the best reassurances stem from exuding an air of confidence rather than mouthing words of comfort. He felt her fingers tighten as the approach signs to Hamilton loomed ahead and he regretfully released her hand to negotiate the curved exit ramp.

'Where do I go from here?'

'Turn left at the first crossroads.'

'Rosanna,' Angus sighed pulling over to the side of the road.

Turning to look at her, he took the trembling hand. 'If you don't look as if you love me, they won't either.'

'Don't be silly Angus. You know I love you. It's just that….'

'That what Darling? Am I too old or too tall? Are you afraid of disappointing them?'

'No…. never that! My family is so outspoken….'

'Rosanna please stop torturing yourself. Childhood habits die hard sometimes. They don't control you or your emotions.'

'Angus, I am not concerned about me. I love my family but I don't want them to hurt you with anything they say or do.'

He reached across to pull her closer and kiss the trembling lips. 'They can't hurt me sweetheart. I've survived all these years alone and now I have you beside me. That's all that matters.' Releasing her he added, 'Come on! Let's get going before I change my mind and head for the nearest motel. You're far too tempting in that dress.'

Rosanna ran nervous fingers down the front of her silky light weight patterned dress.

Angus' words could shift her emotions in a heartbeat. She could feel her breasts straining against the material aching for his touch. Her response was not lost on him. She weighed the options and knew it was just a tease. 'You're right. Let's go! Home!'

An hour later, Rosanna knew the worst was over. Both her parents welcomed their daughter's new boyfriend into their home with guarded but respectful courtesy. Domenic and

Tina arrived soon after. A warning look from his sister sent the eldest son out to the backyard to get acquainted with his prospective brother-in-law, while Tina and Rosanna sat in the kitchen talking.

'How's the job Tina?'

'Didn't you hear that I gave it up?' she announced proudly. 'Dom and I are having another baby.'

'Five Tina? How will you manage?'

'Don't worry. I'll be fine but I want to hear about your guy. He's pretty skinny. Mama will want to feed him.'

'Yes and he'll want to eat. He used to do long distance running. He looks thin but he's really very fit.'

'What's he talking to Mama for? She doesn't speak English. She can't understand anything he says.'

Rosanna turned around to look out the window into the backyard. Sure enough, her mother and Angus had walked over to the vegetable garden. She could see her mother pointing out the lush tomatoes destined for bottles of delicious pasta sauces. They were talking like old friends. Rosanna frowned.

'Mama does understand a lot more than she lets on. She is able to speak a few words. Angus is very understanding. He will make her comfortable.'

Tina was skeptical, but said nothing more as other family members arrived. Rosanna and Angus seemed to be part of a conspiracy to keep them apart. Everyone wanted to meet the new guy. Angus laughed a lot with them. Even

Domenic, who initially looked cautious, relaxed. Naturally, the children flocked to him.

During the afternoon, a look passed between Rosanna and her mother. There had been no time for words but the daughter gave a sigh of relief, for she knew her mother accepted Angus. Only her father's feelings remained elusive. The old man stayed away from his eldest daughter, seeming to avoid a confrontation.

∞

Dinner was ready by early afternoon. It was impossible to feed the entire family indoors so several card tables had been set up end to end in the backyard allowing the family to sit down together for the first time in many months.

It was a lovely feast of Italian food completely prepared by Anna in honour of her daughter. The happy pair sat in the centre of the long table. After the food was consumed, amid laughter, jokes and family stories, a large fruitcake covered in a cream cheese icing was placed on the table in front of them. Before they proceeded to cut the cake, Angus appealed for quiet as he wished to say something. Rosanna threw him a questioning look but he smiled at her before speaking, haltingly, in beautiful, Roman Italian to the surprised members of the family.

'Mr. and Mrs. Amadeo' he began nodding to her parents and avoiding the bulging eyes of his fiancée. 'Not long ago I gave up on the idea of marriage thinking that I would never find a woman who was beautiful inside and out, intelligent, caring and yet so utterly feminine that she could embody all things men seek in a wife. When I met Rosanna I knew that she was all of these things and I offer my thanks to her parents.'

Murmurs of approval floated around the table as the family raised their glasses to toast Tonio and Anna. There was a beaming smile from Anna. Tonio remained resolute. Dom appeared flustered obviously getting an earful from his impatient wife for his own inability to be more romantic. Luke and Terry, recently married, were moved by the words. The children giggled amused that old people could be so silly when they were in love.

Rosanna was about to get up to seal his declaration with a kiss when Angus smiled returning her to her seat with another negative nod.

'Well,' she thought. *'He certainly is talkative all of a sudden. And where did he learn to speak Italian like that'* she queried silently. *'Why didn't he tell me before? When I think of what I said that first day in the kitchen and then….Oh My God, that night…he understood everything!'*

Rosanna felt her cheeks grow hot. Angus saw the look and knew her Latin temperament was about to explode. Hastily grabbing her hand and giving it a gentle squeeze he bent over to remind her, sotto voce, that he was on trial with her family. He disguised it with a peck on the cheek and she subsided with apparent meekness.

Angus loved her when she flew into those tantrums but he could love her better when they were alone. Resuming his narrative, the family quieted.

'Years ago, I was asked by a colleague to assist a young girl, who was orphaned after a very bad disaster in Italy. She was being cared for by a Canadian missionary team. Even though she survived the earthquake, she was desperately ill and needed treatment at the children's hospital where I was a resident. With much support, we were able to bring her to Canada, but we couldn't save her. For that year in which she struggled for life, she was as dear to me and my family as any of my parent's children or foster children.

She stayed very close to me and often made me promise to wait for her to grow up so we could be married. When she finally understood that she would not live long however, she told me, in that prophetic way of little children, that I would never be happy until I found a woman who looked just like her. She was right. Twelve years after Annie's death, I found a new life with Rosanna.' He paused before turning to the senior couple before him.

'Il signor e la signora Amadeo, con il suo permesso vorrei sposare sua figlia,' he concluded smiling with a slight bow in the direction of her parents.

Everyone at the table sat silent. Anna nodded. She had already given her blessing. All eyes were on Tonio who rose slowly. He held the eyes of the man who dared to seek his daughter's hand. Tonio looked Angus up and down, noting with some pride the well tailored beige pants, the open neck shirt, the simple gold signet ring adorning his hand, the brown leather belt and shoes.

His Italian, he thought, although not fluent was passably good. That he loved Rosanna was obvious. His profession was excellent. Making his way slowly around the table he stood very proudly beside his daughter, not in the least intimidated by Angus' height. Tonio smiled before taking his daughter's hand and placed it symbolically in the hand of the man who would be responsible for her care and happiness for the rest of her life. He told Angus in no uncertain terms it was expected. Softening his voice somewhat he said, 'Benvenuto alla nostra familia'.

Amid the cheers and shouts, Rosanna rose to kiss her *fidanzato*. She wasn't totally satisfied. 'A word with you please, Angus?' she hissed into his ear when he released her.

Those who missed Angus' sheepish look and Rosanna's stormy brows thought that the tall doctor was hustling his eager fiancée to some quiet spot to present her with a ring. She entered the house with Angus following meekly behind her. At the end of a short hallway she pulled him into a bedroom. Everything about it was so obviously hers.

'I don't think this is a good idea Rosanna.' Angus was nervous about being alone with her in a bedroom knowing that an anxious and protective father and brother were just a few feet away.

'How could you embarrass me like that? I didn't know you could speak Italian. When I think of all the things I said, exposing myself in my weakest moments. How could you Angus? You should have told me,' she repeated her voice rising, not so much in anger as frustration. Angus wasn't paying attention. He had seen her photographs on the wall and held up a hand to stop her verbal onslaught. He peered myopically at the raven haired beauty smiling angelically in her lacy, white bridal-looking confirmation gown.

Rosanna knew when to hold her tongue. She really didn't want to fight with him. She loved Angus too much and felt too happy about the day's outcome to berate him whether fairly or unfairly. '*What does it matter anyway?*' she thought watching Angus. He seemed to be mesmerized by the portrait on the wall. *'It I couldn't speak Italian he would have understood me in English anyway, because I can't hold my tongue or my temper.'* The wry acknowledgement brought a smile to her face, just as Angus turned around from his contemplation of her youthful features.

'You really did resemble Annie. If she hadn't been so thin......' Angus left the rest unsaid. He held Rosanna's shoulders, searching her face as he often did. She wondered why but continued to hold her peace, knowing intuitively that Angus wanted to say something.

'Annie was Italian, from the south, like many of my childhood neighbors. It was Colleen, who didn't have children, as you know, who changed the name to Annie when her Scottish accent got the better of her. She spent so much time with Annie that the name stuck. I am sure you are aware that she used to be the head nurse in pediatrics until her husband died.'

Angus was silent. He wanted to say something else. The thought eluded him at first. He was sidetracked by the adult beauty of the woman in front of him. He frowned.

'Bad thoughts?'

'No, bad memory.'

'You were talking about Annie.'

'Oh yes. Annie could not speak English but most children who are sick say very little anyway. You have to observe their reactions closely to know what hurts from what doesn't. It was more essential for me to be able to speak to her, which I did by improving my own rudimentary Italian but I never really fully developed the facility for understanding everything especially the rapidly spoken dialects' he added pointedly.

'Angus, mi amore, it wouldn't really have mattered anyway. I just get these tantrums sometimes. However,' she said winding her arms around his neck and reaching up for a kiss, *ti amo caro*. Do you understand that?'

'Even if I didn't, I see love reflected in your eyes and my heart understands.' Unmindful of the family waiting patiently, the happy couple kissed deeply knowing the future was secured by the prophecy of love from a blessed little girl.

Epilogue

The sheer window curtains waved softly inwards pushed by a gentle breeze redolent with the scent of the nearby Ionian Sea. Both the fragrances and the movement drew Rosanna like a beacon, enticing her to experience the sights and smells of this seaport, which her mother Anna had called home. She slipped out easily from under the light sheet, trying not to disturb her husband of just a few days.

Their frenetic efforts to plan the wedding and an exciting honeymoon left them exhausted. Being much more resilient than her hardworking husband, Rosanna didn't mind sleeping in fits and starts. Years of night work enabled her to feel refreshed after the shortest cat nap. The deep well of happiness generated by the love in her heart put lightness in her whole being.

As she made her way to the window seat, the sun was just rising, casting a glow over the maritime port of Ortigia. From the hotel room, Rosanna could catch a glimpse of the city where her mother met and married Antonio Castelo di Amadeo. Anna Palermo sacrificed a traditional courtship and white wedding in exchange for making the momentous decision to travel halfway around the world with an ambitious dreamer.

Antonio had been abandoned in the post war years. He grew up in a church funded orphanage under the tutelage of the nuns. What was lost in family support, he made up with a thirst for knowledge, adventure and challenge. Anna was young, impressionable and the second of five children in a poverty stricken family, struggling to make ends meet. She was only too happy to take her chances with the daring man who stole her heart. Leaving Italy with Antonio meant that she would leave her family behind forever. Nearly forty years later, Rosanna was reversing their footsteps by bringing her husband to see the land of her ancestors.

The new bride had been to Italy many times, mostly tourist spots, but her heart was on a mission to fulfill the prophecy of her own amazing love story.

She listened for any sound from the bed, but Angus slept on, oblivious to the physical absence of his wife. She knew he would soon miss her. Their love had been a raging, unquenchable fire. Its intensity and power challenged them every day to make it real in the mundane world in which they lived. Taking a moment to turn her thoughts away from the intensity of their love, she reflected instead on her wedding day.

Rosanna held her ground against family wishes. She had been determined to marry as soon as possible. Anna had been worried and dismayed by the haste, wanting her first born daughter to have what she missed: the wedding of a lifetime. Rosanna balked at the unnecessary expense and delay. Instead she inveigled the priest in Hamilton to allow her to marry after another couple cancelled a ceremony booked for early spring. She and Angus were ready. Seven months after his extraordinary proposal, with no sign of an unplanned pregnancy, Anna relaxed her vigilance. As she and her husband walked with their daughter down the aisle, tears filled her eyes for what might have been, was real.

Of all the events marking the special day, most of the guests remembered the divergent music. The organ pipes of the century-old, Catholic Church rang out in-between the sounds of a lonely bagpipe, played by Reginald Howard, Angus' father. Her husband-to-be wore the full dress kilt of the MacGregor clan and stood proudly beside his 'best man' and best friend, Morag. She wore a green silky dress, with a shawl made of the clan tartan draped over her right shoulder. To compliment her fiancé's 'best man', Rosanna asked her brother to stand with her. Once he recovered from the shock, Dominic, accepted his sister's request, with the hope that his pregnant wife would give birth well before or long after the wedding day. To complete the unusual turn around, Rosanna's brothers stood with her while Megan and Tuyet joined Morag at Angus' side.

The early April morning was as beautiful as anyone could have imagined. The only jarring spot had been the absence of Angus' brother Ian. The minister could not leave his missionary post in South America and Angus did not push, for the brothers were still unable to reconcile the hurt which passed between them.

At the reception afterward, Angus' parents accepted her into the family by performing a draping of the family tartan, symbolizing that she was now indeed a member of the MacGregor clan. Rosanna had been happier than she could ever remember.

At some point in the evening festivities, Morag pulled her aside to fulfill the promise of a story. She talked at length about 'Annie' whose wonderful spirit had been instrumental in driving the love between Angus and Rosanna. Her narrative, as promised, gave the new bride, much food for thought. There were many details which Angus had not known at the time. As a senior resident he was busy with so many aspects of care. Morag went on to explain that he had worried about Annie but generally had little time beyond her daily progress to be involved in her life. Much of the social support for the orphan was left to the Howard family and other members of the Presbyterian church who helped to fund her care. Morag, in discussing the story with her new sister in law, suggested a plan. She hoped the new bride would be agreeable. Rosanna instinctively knew that she had to act on the information received.

After a transatlantic flight and a two day stop over in Rome, Rosanna and Angus had traveled down to the island of Sicily to spend the bulk of their much needed ten day honeymoon. He would be returning home to resume his intense research work. Rosanna would continue with her own hospital committee activity and several exciting projects in the nursing office. Within a year she hoped to start a family.

As the sun brought more and more light into the room, Angus began to stir. It didn't take long for him to note the absence of his wife. He opened one sleepy eye, searching for her dark hair.

Rosanna felt his awakening energy and beckoned for him to join her at the cushioned window seat. She shifted slightly to allow his long legs to wrap around her before settling her body against his. She leaned her head back on his shoulder. At those moments, she felt her world to be complete. They sat in quiet contemplation of the view. It was sometime before Rosanna broke the companionable silence.

'I can't imagine how my mother made the trip to Canada, Angus. I always wondered if she was afraid. She must have loved my father very much to take such a chance.' Rosanna sighed thinking, with pride, of her parents strength and longevity which brought stability to the lives of her children. 'Mama had virtually no education, so little life experience and very limited skills and yet she achieved so much.'

'Love can remove many boundaries, including and especially those built by fear.'

Rosanna nodded. Her philosophic husband was always able to reduce the most complex issues to the simple common denominator called love.

'Are we going to look for her old homestead?'

'That sounds so strange, Angus. I don't think Mama had anything as sophisticated as that. She may have had a well established home but they were poor. She was barely seventeen when she met my father and married him in a borrowed dress. The day she got on that boat with Papa was her final goodbye to everything she had known. By the time I was starting school, Mama could hardly remember the family she left behind.'

'Then what are we going to do?' he asked giving her a tight hug to acknowledge the impact of sharing a very personal moment of nostalgia. 'Just so that you know…. I'm happy to stay right here with you.'

'We are taking a small driving tour today. Nothing elaborate.'

Angus grunted and drew his wife even closer. He didn't really care about much else. The loving husband would be content to hold his wife all day, listening to her stories.

∞

After a mid morning breakfast, the hired car arrived and drove them up the coast road to Catania just an hour away. Rosanna said little. She and Angus held hands. They sought each other's company in conversation, just as often as they sat quietly and looked out over the sea, which rose, from time to time, into their vision. The ride had been pleasurable.

The driver eventually stopped in front of a small well kept home, typical of the area. Each house was painted white with bright blue shutters. The view down the road was picture perfect.

'Is there someone you know living here?' Angus inquired.

'No, my mother's family lived right in Ortigia. This is another family I want you to meet. I hope you will be surprised and pleased.'

Rosanna and Angus quickly climbed out of the car. A young boy with dark hair opened the door and stared at the unusual couple who were approaching.

Rosanna's last words came back to mind as her own face registered complete surprise. The young face in front of her was a replica of her younger brother! Startled by the resemblance, she spoke rapidly in Italian asking for the boy's mother. He invited them inside, calling for his mother at the same time. Both Angus and Rosanna noted that he had some disabilities despite his cheerful demeanour.

As they waited, the eyes of the youngster watched them curiously. Angus and Rosanna looked around, seeing the knick-knacks and religious artifacts that decorated the room. Both turned as footsteps were heard moving along the upper floor and down the stairs. A woman's leg appeared. Deep scarring showed along its lines. Once her face came into view, the Canadian couple could not hold back the gasp, anymore than the woman standing at the entrance to the small living room, could prevent her wide open eyes from registering shock. Her gaze was not directed at Angus whom she knew from Morag's photos, but at Rosanna who was a living embodiment of her daughter.

The astonishment on both sides was intense.

'Senor, Doctor Gus! Welcome to my home. Giovanna pulled her eyes away from Rosanna and drew Angus to her. She held out her arms for a lingering hug. Tears filled her eyes.

'I didn't know about you. I thought you had died in the earthquake.' Angus was moved by the unexpected meeting.

'I was sick for too long after the birth of Mateo. I didn't know that Anunziata was with you. I thought she died with her father.'

'And she thought you had died with her grandmother. I wished I could have saved her but how did you know about me?'

'Miss Mora!'

'My sister?'

'She asked people from your church to return to Irpina and find someone who knew my daughter. Since I was not well known in the village the search was difficult. It was a year after the quake before I could even speak. By then, my son was almost a year old. He didn't know me at all. My child, my beautiful girl, Anunziata, died without knowing she had a brother.'

'I am sorry for your loss. Giovanna. Annie was a wonderful child. Every day she told me I would marry a woman who looked just like her. This lady, who does remind me so much of her, is my wife Rosanna.'

Giovanna held out her arms to Rosanna. Without hesitation, they embraced, holding each other, generating tears. There was much to talk about. Rosanna had known where she was taking Angus. The intent of the visit was to surprise him. She understood that Giovanna would want to know about her daughter. After a period of getting acquainted, Angus was asked questions about the last year in the life of the little girl.

Over a light meal, the pediatrician took time to explain to Giovanna the status of 'Annie's' heart and why it didn't function. He drew a simple heart shaped square and explained how the blood normally flows and how the tubes leading in and out were changed, turned around, and had blockages which made the heart work harder. Giovanna nodded her understanding.

'Her heart was too big. Working too hard?'

"Yes, but her heart was also filled with love. She was a beautiful child giving to us as much love as we gave her.' Angus spoke in his lovely Italian, making the conversation very personal for Giovanna.

They were interrupted by a sound upstairs. Giovanna excused herself. 'I must see to her. I will be right back.'

Angus looked at his wife, loving her smiling face.

'Thank you for this Rosanna. I can't tell you how much closure this brings to me.'

'And to her as well. Morag was never sure if she should tell you that Annie's mother survived.'

'I can understand why she would withhold that from me. My life was already so complicated. She knew I would immediately come here. This is the right time for us to be here my love.'

Giovanna soon returned to her guests apologizing for the distraction. Mama is very old. I can't leave her for long. Please Rosanna. Tell me about you?'

Rosanna was comfortable with the energy of this kindly woman who, appeared to be slightly older than Angus. She related some of her family and work information.

'Your parents are from Sicily?'

'My father, I don't know. He is unaware of his origins however, my mother comes from Ortigia'.

'Ah, me too.'

Rosanna was puzzled. She thought that her hostess had been born in Irpina where the quake had taken place.

'Oh no, after our marriage, Mateo brought me from Ortigia to stay with his parents in Irpina so I could have help with Anunziata. You see, he was a sailor and away from home often. He worried about me and his little girl. He worked hard until the day he was injured on a ship. I never thought I would lose him to the earthquake. He was such a good man,' she concluded shaking her head.

'It is wonderful that you are able to care for your mother-in-law.'

'That is not my husband's mother upstairs. She did not survive the quake. It is my mother.'

Giovanna shed a few tears. Clearly the day had healed some wounds and opened others.

'Do you have any other brothers or sisters?' Rosanna asked hoping to deflect some of the grief.

'I was the last pregnancy of my mother. She called me her miracle. It was long after her normal time and she didn't expect to become pregnant ever again. I had some much older brothers and sisters who I never knew. Mama lived with one of my brothers until he died. All the others are gone now except a brother in the north, who is a priest and a sister in America who is too rich to care about me.

I don't have a lot, and yet I am content. Much sadness has come my way but my daughter was my own miracle. She brought me much comfort while Mateo was away. When I meet people like you, today I know she watches me and her brother Mateo. I feel that she is in Heaven with her father and she is safe.'

Giovanna crossed herself and gathered her young son to her.

'Sing to me Mama,' he begged. It was apparent that the ritual of crying and singing was a routine in the house.

Rosanna recognized the custom, thinking it to be completely Sicilian.

Giovanna smiled. With a shrug of her shoulders, she apologized to her guests. 'It makes him happy.'

In a softly sweet soprano voice, she sang O Mio Babbino Caro. Angus and Rosanna were moved to tears by the beautiful voice. A question hovered in Rosanna's mind for she felt profoundly connected to this woman.

'What is your mother's name Giovanna?'

'Rosa Palermo.'

'My grandmother!'

There was no great astonishment for the resemblance was too close to be coincidental. In time, Rosanna would be able to correct any misunderstandings which Giovanna harboured about her long lost sister. Rosanna could not begin to imagine the untold joy her own mother would feel at the news. To know that her mother, a sister, and a brother were found seemed to be an unimaginable gift.

Rosanna looked at her loving husband. She spoke softly in English. 'How is it possible Angus that we could come to this moment, after we have already been so blessed?'

Even before he opened his mouth, she pre-empted him with the words,

'I suspect love, is your answer.'

My very grateful thanks to all the wonderful people I have known in my life who in one way or another helped to create and shape the characters here. I also give thanks to my muse, a wonderful friend, passed into the Summerland of death whose energy remains behind to encourage me to tell my heart stories.